The Wilbur Stories & More

stories by

Barry Vitcov

Finishing Line Press
Georgetown, Kentucky

The Wilbur Stories
& More

ACKNOWLEDGMENTS

Ben	Scarlet Leaf Review	January 2020
Max	Scarlet Leaf Review	February 2020
Trapped	Scarlet Leaf Review	September 2020
Abby Learns to Play the Tuba	Finding the Birds	May 2020

Publisher: Leah Huete de Maines
Editor: Christen Kincaid
Cover Art: William E. Saltzsen
Author Photo: William E. Saltzsen
Cover Design: Elizabeth Maines McCleavy

Order online: www.finishinglinepress.com
              also available on amazon.com

Author inquiries and mail orders:
Finishing Line Press
P. O. Box 1626
Georgetown, Kentucky 40324
U. S. A.

Table of Contents

The Wilbur Stories

More Stories

To my sister Paula
for her enthusiastic support...

...and to a small and valued group of friends
who read my stories and kept me motivated...

...and to Matt, a wall builder extraordinaire!

Thank you!

The Wilbur Stories

The Flower Bandit

Sal walks the same three-mile loop every morning, just after dawn breaks, looking for a new flower to pick. He carefully selects one that grabs his attention; one that he has not previously selected. It's important that he not choose the same blossom twice. His goal is to notice and catalog each unique flower on the route he walks each morning. He relishes routine and constancy. He finds comfort in sameness punctuated by surprise.

First, he notices the flower's color and then the shape. Once he has made his choice, he looks around to check if anyone spots him before using his Swiss Army knife's scissors to clip the specimen. He prefers that his daily task be done surreptitiously. He doesn't want to deal with any conflict that may come from a resident objecting to his flower plucking.

After he returns home, he places the flower on his desk's black blotter and arranges it so that the natural light streaming in from the adjacent window illuminates it to his liking. He uses a small Canon PowerShot camera to take a photograph, which he uploads to his computer. After using a photo editing application to achieve just the right appearance, Sal uploads the picture to Facebook and Instagram with the simple message, "Today's flower for you…" So far, he has posted seventy-six pictures, three more than the number of his Facebook friends. He has no followers on Instagram.

At six feet and 156 pounds, forty-two-year-old Sal walks like a cipher. He wears his straight black hair shoulder length. As he moves with a bobbing gait, he looks like a cheerleader's pom-pom. Clothing is never a difficult choice, as he always wears a black T-shirt, black jeans, and black tennis shoes. His clothing doesn't reflect his optimistic personality and he has no need to dress for a job because he works from home as a customer service representative for an online retailer.

On the seventy-seventh morning of his flower search, Wilbur changed Sal's routine. Wilbur was nine and lived in the largest house, a grand white Colonial, along Sal's daily walk. He was an only child and home-schooled by his single mother, whose divorce left her with a comfortable fortune. Sal never noticed Wilbur sitting on the front porch when he walked by each morning. Wilbur's front yard had virtually no flowers. The wide lawn was bordered by a finely trimmed Boxwood hedge and the area around the porch was filled with varieties of Hosta, ferns and showy grasses. Considering the house's style, Sal thought there ought to be azaleas and rhododendrons brightening up the planting beds. He would have also included a mix of mums, daisies, and marigolds. There needed to be splashes of color.

Wilbur sat in a large, white wicker chair unnoticed by Sal until he stood, walked down the serpentine Flagstone path to the sidewalk and said, "I watch you walk by my house every morning."

Sal stopped and looked down at a slightly pudgy child who clearly needed exercise and probably a diet free of junk food. Wilbur looked up at Sal with a smile and nervous hands. His hair was sheared short, and he was still wearing flannel pajamas and moccasin-style slippers.

"You watch, do you?" questioned Sal.

"You come by at almost exactly the same time every morning. I check the time on my Apple watch," which was clearly visible on Wilbur's left wrist.

"You're keeping track of me," said Sal. "What's your name?"

Sal observed that Wilbur seemed lost and uncertain, but his eyes appeared inquisitive and there was an unused intelligence about him. Sal thought this boy might be a lot like himself when he was a youngster. Sal had been a little overweight before his teenage years when he grew tall and slim like his father. Even then he had a penchant for collecting things: stamps, matchbook covers, butterflies, and for over six months a ball of aluminum foil. His mother finally made him dispose of the foil in the recycling bin. "It's beginning to smell up your bedroom, Salvador, get rid of it."

"I'm Wilbur."

"Shouldn't you be getting ready for school?"

"I'm homeschooled," answered Wilbur. "What are you doing?"

"I like to walk before work. I like to pick a new flower every day."

Wilbur thought a moment before grinning and saying, "You're like a robber. You are a flower bandit."

"I never thought of it that way, but you could be right."

Wilbur laughed. "Why do you do it?"

"I like flowers and I like looking for beautiful things to brighten my day," replied Sal. "Do you have any collections?"

Like Wilbur, Sal was an only child born into a loving family that used to be called middle class. He resembled his father in build and quirkiness. He didn't quite have his mother's fortitude and firmness. His father had worked for the post office and his mother part-time at a local Hallmark shop. His mother often said she liked the cards but hated the syrupy movies. He was expected to do well in school, keep up with his chores, and spend his free time however he chose. His newly retired father enjoyed pickle ball and historical fiction. His mother continued working at the same shop for the current minimum wage just as she had thirty years prior. She always said, "It's not about the money. It's about getting out of the house."

Wilbur's weekday routine was getting up just after sunrise, grabbing a juice box from the refrigerator and a handful of fig newtons, and enjoying them on the front porch regardless of the weather. His mother called him into breakfast at 9:00 and his first tutor arrived at 10:00 for two hours of English, history, and art. He fixed his own lunch, which was usually peanut butter and jelly, chips, and another handful of fig newtons. At 1:00 the second tutor arrived for two hours of math and science. After working with his tutors, he completed his homework before settling in with the television before dinner. Typically, his mother ordered out for dinner. He and his mother ate together, and they discussed his lessons. His mother took great interest in what he was learning. She had been an excellent student throughout high school and college where she earned a business degree that she never used. She married a wealthy hedge fund manager, had Wilbur five years later and was amicably divorced after ten years. Wilbur visited his father one weekend per month. On the other weekends, if his mother didn't have some sort of outing for them to do together, he could be found at the nearby park playing with friends. He gravitated towards other kids who lived in similar familial situations, except they all went to public or private schools. Wilbur was an easy-going boy with an approachable affect.

Wilbur thought about Sal's question and replied, "I collect rocks."

"Where do you find them?"

"Around."

"Might you be a rock bandit, Wilbur?"

The front door opened, and Wilbur's mother called out, "Wilbur, who are you talking to?"

"The flower bandit," called back Wilbur.

Wilbur's mother walked down to where they were standing. She was an attractive woman who walked with grace and determination. Her dark hair was cut short and clearly by a high-end salon. She approached with a smile and said, "So you're the fellow Wilbur talks about. You walk by our home every morning about the same time. I'm Eli, by the way. And you are?"

"Sal."

"He's a flower bandit," interjected Wilbur. "He collects flowers without asking."

"Well, that's true. I look for one flower each day that I photograph and post on Facebook. I don't think I'm breaking any laws."

Eli laughed and said, "I don't think so either. Wilbur collects rocks. He has quite a pile in the backyard."

Sal, Wilbur and Eli spoke for a few more minutes. Eli apologized for Wilbur's forwardness, but Sal said he wasn't offended at all. He told Eli that he appreciated anyone who liked to collect things. He felt a sense of comradeship with Wilbur. He was about to bid goodbye when Wilbur asked his mother if he could walk a bit with Sal. Eli objected at first out of concern for knowing so little about Sal. Then she gave permission for Wilbur to walk the next two blocks before he would need to return home. She watched as they walked away, Wilbur still in his pajamas and slippers. About half a block away she saw Sal stoop to cut a flower. Wilbur also bent over and seemed to pick up a small rock. He turned around and speed walked home while Sal continued on his way.

"Look what I found." Wilbur showed his mother a small grey stone with milky striations running through it. "Sal, took a purple flower."

For the next three months, Wilbur met Sal on the sidewalk. Eli allowed Wilbur to walk further and further each day. Sal was sure to alter his original walk so that he could drop Wilbur back at his house before he returned to his own. Wilbur began carrying a small, spiralbound notebook and yellow pencil where he would record each day's flower and rock collection. If Sal had a flower in hand by the time they met, he'd anxiously ask to see and make note of it. They were forming a collector's bond. Sal quickly learned that Wilbur was a very curious and precocious child. He was impressed with his observational talents and his ability to write accurate descriptions. When he had difficulty finding the words to describe his rocks, Sal helped. Jagged, flaky, coarse and silky were a few of the words added to Wilbur's vocabulary.

Eli was pleased with the time Wilbur was spending with Sal. She believed Sal had become a good male adult role model; one that Wilbur's father failed to achieve. The math and science tutor was very happy with Wilbur keeping a rock journal. He brought Wilbur a child's rock and mineral guide, which quickly became dog-eared.

One morning, Eli asked if Sal would like to join them for breakfast. He declined because he needed to return home, take care of his photography tasks and then get to work.

"How about a weekend morning?" asked Eli.

"Sure. That would be fine."

Sal became a regular breakfast guest on those weekends when Wilbur did not stay with his father. Eli told Sal he was still welcome on those weekends when Wilbur was at his father's, but Sal still declined.

"It's just breakfast, Sal. Nothing more," said Eli.

"I understand. I just don't want to confuse things," said Sal.

Eli wondered what Sal meant, but didn't pursue it any further. Even though she was not intending anything beyond a pleasant breakfast and conversation, she thought Sal might be in another relationship. He never talked about himself and seemed reserved and introspective.

Eli informed Sal that Wilbur's tenth birthday was approaching and that she'd have something special for Saturday's breakfast. When Sal met Wilbur for their walk that day, Wilbur was dressed just like Sal in all black.

"I've decided that black is the color for serious collectors."

"Well, I guess I'll take that as a compliment, Wilbur. And I have something for you on your special day." Sal handed Wilbur a small package wrapped in a floral print paper.

Eli appeared and called out, "Leave your gift with me until breakfast and enjoy your hunt."

Over the months Sal noticed how Wilbur had become much more self-assured. He no longer had nervous hands and he had developed a much more serious interest and focus as a collector.

They returned with Sal holding an orange and yellow tea rose and Wilbur with an ordinary looking piece of pea gravel, which he claimed to be different from all other pea gravel specimens. For his birthday, they had instant oatmeal and an immense store-bought carrot cake with "Happy Tenth Birthday, Wilbur" written in blue icing.

"We're having a party in the park later with some of Wilbur's friends, and we'll take the remainder of the cake with other goodies," explained Eli. "Wilbur, go ahead and open the gift from Sal."

Wilbur unwrapped the package to find a journal with the title "Wilbur Rocks" stitched into the cloth cover.

"Notice it says "Wilbur Rocks", not "Wilbur's Rocks.""

"What's the difference?" asked Wilbur.

"It's called a play on words. You rock, Wilbur."

"Oh, I get it. I rock!"

"Yes, you do, Wilbur."

One Saturday well into Wilbur's tenth year, over a breakfast of toaster waffles and cranberry juice, Wilbur said, "I think it's interesting that rocks are like fingerprints."

"You mean no two are the same, Wilbur?"

"Exactly." Wilbur paused and thought some more. "That goes for flowers and snowflakes and lots of other things in nature. It's interesting."

"Nature is filled with uniqueness," said Sal. "We are all different. You're not a teenager yet. When you are, you'll probably feel like you want to be like everyone else. When I felt that way, my father used to tell me that you'll be an adult when you appreciate your own uniqueness and the uniqueness of others. And especially when you take a genuine interest in those differences."

Wilbur turned to his mother and said, "I think what Sal means is that we're both bandits, but he looks for flowers and I look for rocks."

Eli commented, "Perhaps."

Wilbur Builds a Wall

It was smoke season in the valley. Every summer Bear City residents waited for the first fire in the mountains, near or as far away as 100 miles, to fill the valley with smoke. Bear City is located at the end of a picturesque valley between two long mountain ranges. Prevailing winds push forest smoke into the valley causing senior citizens to stay inside and young folk to frolic in the outdoors and dare the smoke to harm them. Everybody in-between has jobs and family responsibilities and make do the best they can. Bear City has one major river dividing the town into regions, the Westside, with most of the town's shopping and residential area nestled up against a sloping hillside, and the Eastside occupying the flatter, mostly agricultural region often subject to the river's winter and spring floods. The area is popular with hunters, fly fishers, and artists seeking natural beauty and quietude. There is also an uber abundance of chiropractors, new-age life coaches, holistic medical practitioners, bicycle builders, boutique farmers, well-to-do retirees, financial investment advisors, small bed and breakfast establishments, and attorneys who mostly specialize in wills and trusts.

It was mid-July and fortunately no fires; hence, no smoke. Wilbur sat at a booth in Pop's Donuts and Coffee sipping black coffee and munching on an old-fashioned donut when Sal entered, said hello to Phyllis who owned the shop with her husband Jack, ordered a medium latte and sat across from Wilbur. It had been their morning routine ever since Sal had retired as the director of online services for a major retailer. Their friendship went back thirty years when Sal and Wilbur found a unique friendship as obsessive collectors, Sal finding a daily flower to photograph and post online and Wilbur collecting rocks. Wilbur had just turned forty-two, the same age as Sal when they first met. At almost seventy-three, Sal was still gaunt and sported a bushy head of gray hair, which for some inexplicable reason, turned increasingly curly with each gray strand. He appeared to some as a very thin, less-of-a-genius Einstein.

"What's doing today?" asked Sal.

"I'm still working on the wall for Mr. and Mrs. Watson. It's a long one and I'm still gathering river rocks for it. I hope to finish it before winter."

Wilbur had developed a reputation as Bear City's Andy Goldsworthy, the British sculpture famous for his imaginative stonework. Wilbur always had a fascination for rocks. He graduated from a college far from home with a major in geology and an art minor with an emphasis on architectural drawing. He ended up pursuing a master's degree in architecture and, through several internships, found work as a junior architect back in Bear City. He was living at home with his mother Eli when one day she insisted that he do something with the huge rock pile that had accumulated in the back yard from his collecting days with Sal. That's when he built his first wall, a low serpentine wall across a portion of the front yard planting bed. With Sal's assistance, he planted a variety of colorful plants. Sal was ecstatic about color finally gracing the front of Eli's house. Passersby began noticing the wall and offered Wilbur work to build walls for them. Before long, Wilbur resigned from his architect's job and worked full-time designing and constructing walls.

From time to time, he partnered with Sal, who was working less in anticipation of retirement, when his clients wanted the job to include a garden installation. Wilbur explained to his growing list of clients that they would need to be patient and expect delays, but no one ever complained.

"You know, Wilbur, you don't need to collect all the rocks you need to build the Watson's wall. You could order some river rocks from a supplier," said Sal.

"You're right, but it wouldn't be the same," responded Wilbur. "Have you ever heard of the Tor House in Carmel? Poet Robinson Jeffers helped to build that stone house and adjoining tower with much of the stone gathered from the nearby beach. There's something about the gathering process that makes the building much more meaningful."

Sal and Wilbur were quiet for a moment before Sal asked, "Are you a poet or a wall builder?"

"Maybe a bit of both. The idea and design are poetry, but the stone is labor."

Wilbur had been working on the Watson's wall for almost three months and he estimated another three before it would be completed. The wall stretched almost 300 yards bisecting the property on which there were two identical houses. Mrs. Watson lived in one and Mr. Watson in the other. They had been married close to forty years but didn't live together. Childless, with little in common other than the property, they had a secret understanding. After fifteen years of a seemingly happy marriage rich in civic and social engagement, they built a second home that Mr. Watson moved into. They withdrew from town life, which the town's residents chalked up to quirkiness and never asked either of the Watsons about their newly sudden arrangement. No one knew the source of their income; they only knew that they lived well as they observed frequent FedEx and United Parcel truck deliveries along with their regular grocery shopping at the most expensive gourmet market in Bear City.

Wilbur designed the wall to gently curve around the landscape's natural slopes with a gate about midway down its length. The wall's height would vary from two to three feet and would be determined as Wilbur would say, "In the moment and gracefully." It would be constructed entirely with river rock gathered from a large stretch of riverfront property Wilbur had purchased after the sale of his mother's home. His mother had died after a short battle with ovarian cancer and Wilbur couldn't imagine living in such a grand home. He built a small, two-bedroom cabin on the riverfront property that gave him access to a limitless supply of river rock. He now lived there with his wife Sam and pre-teen daughter Elizabeth.

Wilbur and Sal continued to be collectors. Wilbur's rock collecting now served a different purpose: building walls. Sal still looked for flowers with a look that spoke to him. Over the years, he had collected and catalogued every known flower in the valley. As he had when he first met Wilbur, he no longer walked the same route every morning, but he did take walks in different neighborhoods looking for flowers that he thought interesting in their shape and color. He had also invested in pricey photography equipment allowing for sophisticated manipulation of his photos. He now produced signed and numbered prints that sold for hundreds and sometimes thousands of dollars at art fairs. Sal's wife of almost thirty years was also an accomplished watercolor artist. Wilbur's mother had purchased several of Sally's paintings and Wilbur insisted that Eli invite Sally to one of the weekend breakfasts which she served to him and Sal. Wilbur liked to think that he had facilitated the beginning of Sal's and Sally's romance. Sal and Sally had become well-known as the "Artists S^2" and many of their invitation-only shows were advertised as "New Work From and For the Squared."

Wilbur and Sal continued to sip their coffee and Sal asked, "What piece of the poem will you be building today?"

"I'm at that point where a gap needs to be created for a gate. It's ironic that two people who don't live together and are paying me to build a wall to keep their separateness also want a gate into each other's space." Wilbur smiled while Sal nodded. They had a well-developed silent language of gestures.

"It's their way of being comfortable in their world. Aren't all relationships built with walls and doors? Maybe we coexist through a kind of social osmosis with our own way of filtering communication and relationships."

"What do you mean, Sal?"

"Do you remember when I told you that my father said we become adults when we value our own and each other's uniqueness?"

"Vividly. It's stayed with me all these years."

Sal continued, "I think it also means that in our own unique way we build structures for self-protection and communication. That wall you are building is part of that structure. It's what makes them different."

"Well, Sal, it's wall-building time. I need to get going. See you tomorrow morning."

Wilbur owned a fully restored 1947 Ford one-ton flatbed truck that was always loaded with a collection river rock. The restoration was only mechanical, and the surviving paint was flaking rusty red. The weight of the stone guaranteed a smooth ride as long as he eased it over extreme bumps and potholes. As he drove up Mrs. Watson's driveway, the smoother of the two entrances, he saw Mr. and Mrs. Watson standing where the gate was intended to be placed.

"Wilbur, good to see you," said Mr. Watson. "Mrs. Watson and I have some suggestions about the gate we want to share with you."

Wilbur approached wondering what they might have in mind. The three of them stood at the end of the first half of the wall. Mr. and Mrs. Watson were both in their early sixties. Mrs. Watson, who still insisted on Mrs. rather than Ms., stood slightly taller than her husband. She reminded Wilbur of his mother with her short black hair cut stylishly at a high-end salon. Her posture suggested confidence and she was dressed casually in a white T-shirt and loose-fitting denim pants. Mr. Watson wore a black jumpsuit, which hung evenly and appeared to have been ironed as evidenced by the straight creases down the pant legs. He wore his hair in an old-fashioned butch cut that accentuated his angular face giving him a seriously boyish look. Wilbur knew their first names to be Rebecca and Claude, but they only referred to themselves as Mr. and Mrs. Watson, so Wilbur obliged the courtesy of that more formal address.

Wilbur asked, "What do you have in mind."

Mrs. Watson replied, "Rather than a gate that opens and shuts with a latch and maybe even a lock, we'd prefer an arched opening."

"Yes," added Mr. Watson. "We wish to have a wall with a break that invites easy passage."

Wilbur considered their request while examining the area where the arched opening would be constructed. "I think that would work. This spot is fairly flat and would make it an easier build. How wide would you want it?"

"We'd like to be able to get a small tractor or riding lawn mower through. We're thinking of some extensive landscaping on both sides of the wall with a fairly large area of lawn," said Mrs. Watson.

"And we really don't need two tractors or other duplicate landscaping tools," said Mr. Watson.

"That makes sense," acknowledged Wilbur. "I'll build the second half of the wall before I do the arch and finish the project."

"Thanks, Wilbur, it's really looking good," said Mrs. Watson while her husband nodded in agreement.

Wilbur laid another ten feet of wall before heading home. He parked his truck near the river and began loading more rock for the next day's labor. His daughter Elizabeth walked down to help. Wilbur enjoyed her company and they generally worked quietly together. Elizabeth took after her mother Sam, blond and athletic. However, while Sam was extroverted, Elizabeth was slightly introverted. She wasn't shy, but she knew when to speak up and when to reserve her voice. When she was born, Wilbur and Sam decided to name her after her grandmother and called her Eli at first. On Elizabeth's sixth birthday, she told her parents she wanted to be called Elizabeth.

"Wasn't that grandma's full name?" she asked. Wilbur said it was. "Then I want to have a full name like grandma's." From that moment on, it was always Elizabeth. Wilbur and Sam appreciated their daughter's gumption and spirit. They also admired her early maturity and shared a concern for what it might be like when she became a teenager.

"How's it going with the Watson's wall?"

"They decided they don't want a gate, but an archway instead. Maybe you'd like to help when it's time to build the arch. I could use an extra pair of hands."

"Sure. That would be fun. Maybe I could also help with some of the wall, too."

"You're on. Want to begin tomorrow?"

They continued to load rock onto the truck bed before Sam called them into dinner. Sam was a middle school science teacher, and, during the school year, it was everybody on their own for meals. Wilbur did a fair amount of cooking and Elizabeth helped sometimes. During the summer, however, Sam enjoyed preparing dinners and used much of the fresh produce from the small kitchen garden adjacent to the cabin. They weren't vegetarians but ate little red meat. Mostly it was chicken and often whatever fish were running in the river. Elizabeth had become quite an accomplished fly fisher and was always excited when she had a good morning catch.

They sat around the porch table eating one of Sam's specialties, vegetarian lasagna with a garden salad. Wilbur and Sam sipped a local red wine and Elizabeth drank fizzy water.

"Dad says the Watson's want an archway instead of a gate."

"What do you think that's all about?" asked Sam.

"I'm not sure. And they want it large enough to drive a small tractor through and other shared landscaping equipment. They're planning some extensive landscaping. I wonder if Sal might be interested in helping them select flowers."

Elizabeth said, "It's funny how they live in separate houses, want a wall to keep things apart but an opening large enough to share stuff. Somehow it's weird."

"Sal thinks it's just what makes them different. It's hard to know, but they're sure easy to work for. And I like the way the wall is looking. I think an archway will make it very special. I bet Sal would like to plant climbing roses there."

Wilbur and Elizabeth worked together for the next month and made good headway. Wilbur found that Elizabeth had a good eye for design and made several suggestions that helped to keep the wall moving forward in what Wilbur called a "poetic flow." Mr. and Mrs. Watson would sit on their respective porches watching father and daughter work together. Every few hours or so, one of them would bring down a cold drink and a snack, sometimes simultaneously. Elizabeth enjoyed quiet conversations with both, often times out of Wilbur's earshot.

"Before school starts, I think we ought to build the archway. That's when I can really use your help," said Wilbur.

"Great! I'm looking forward to seeing how that works," replied Elizabeth.

They spent the next week carefully constructing the stone archway using a wooden scaffolding to hold the structure in place until they placed the last of the keystones. The columns and the arch were the only part of the entire project where mortar was used for stability. When they pulled the supporting structure away, Mr. and Mrs. Watson applauded and shouted, "Congratulations! You've really created a masterpiece."

"Dad, that was really something. It all held in place and it's beautiful," remarked Elizabeth on the drive home.

Wilbur felt a flush of pride before saying, "We did it together."

Fall arrived and the wall was finished. Wilbur was sitting with Sal at Pop's enjoying his coffee and a plain old fashioned and Sal his latte. Sal had just come from the Watson's having planted some climbing roses so that they would cover the archway.

"I planted yellow and red roses. They will eventually intertwine and form a colorful display. As it turns out, Mrs. Watson loves red roses and Mr. Watson yellow. They wanted something symbolic of their relationship."

"I guess some walls are intended to separate and others not so much," said Wilbur.

Sal and Sally

Eli and Wilbur watched as Sally hung a watercolor picturing the river that flows through the valley where Bear City is located. Her skill at capturing the movement of water and the surrounding foliage evoked feelings of peace and solitude, a respite from the tensions of the real world. The painting was one of Eli's recent purchases from Sally, a local artist who was rapidly gaining favor among the town's residents as well as a broader audience throughout the region. At one time, she had been an art teacher at the same middle school that Wilbur now attends after being homeschooled during his elementary years. This was the fifth piece of Sally's work that Eli had purchased.

"I believe you now qualify as a primary patron of my work," said Sally.

"Well, I love your watercolors and I'm sure I'll be buying more in the future," replied Eli.

It was a late Saturday morning. Wilbur and Sal had already completed their morning collections. Sal had picked a lustrous purple chicory blossom and Wilbur found a rust-colored stone with black spots that had caught his eye among a pile of bland pea gravel. Wilbur's stone was now part of his growing heap in the backyard. And the rocks had been getting larger and larger as Wilbur's body lost its pudginess and became hard and sinewy just as his voice began to change. He was now able to tote heavier rocks, sometimes picking large chunks of broken concrete, which he claimed he might use in a future project. Eli had served them a Saturday breakfast of Eggo French toast sticks and microwaved Jimmy Dean sausages. Sal had left hours before Sally arrived with the new watercolor.

"Let's have some lunch on the back patio, Sally, I've made some sandwiches and some iced tea."

The three of them sat at the round, glass-topped table under an immense blue umbrella enjoying store-bought deviled ham salad sandwiches and bottled iced tea. Off to the side of the patio was Wilbur's rock pile and beyond an expanse of lawn surrounded by low hedges and a smattering of birch and redbud trees. After eying the rock pile, Sally noticed a yard devoid of colorful plants.

Sally was not a shy person and was often unfiltered with her comments. "That's quite a pile you've got going there, Wilbur. You ought to build something with those rocks."

"I've been thinking about it."

"And Eli, this is a lovely backyard, but it could use some color. You know, like my paintings," suggested Sally.

Wilbur looked at his mother who seemed nonplussed while shaking her head in agreement. "I've been thinking about adding some flowers. You know, Wilbur walks every morning with his friend Sal who collects flower specimens to photograph. He's much older than Wilbur, but, over the last few years, I've grown to trust him. He's almost like a second father to Wilbur."

"Really."

"I know it sounds weird for an older fellow to befriend a young boy, but it's really quite nice. After they finish their weekend collecting walks, Sal will stay for breakfast. During the week they still walk, but Sal has his job and now Wilbur needs to get to school. In fact, you just missed meeting Sal this morning. I think he does some garden work. Maybe I ought to ask him about doing the backyard?"

The next day Sal picked a Madonna lily and Wilbur found a large chunk of concrete that had been tossed on a debris pile where some new construction was just beginning. He liked the smooth top and ragged edges. "I think it looks like Italy, Sal." They continued to walk back to Wilbur's house with Wilbur needing to stop and get a better grip on one of his larger finds. "Sal, mom is thinking about planting some flowers in the backyard."

"That's a good idea."

"Would you be interested in helping?"

"Maybe. It depends on what your mom wants and how much time I have."

"Her artist friend suggested it," said Wilbur.

"Artist friend?" asked Sal.

Wilbur stood still, holding the scrap of concrete in both hands, and said, "Mom has been buying some watercolors from Sally, and, yesterday, at lunch Sally suggested some color would be nice."

When they approached Wilbur's house, Eli was sitting on the front porch holding a red mug. Wilbur informed his mother that Sal might be interested in helping to add some color to the backyard.

"He would, Wilbur?" questioned Eli.

"Maybe," said Sal. "I understand you have an artist friend who suggested it."

Wilbur added, "We ought to invite Sally over for breakfast next Saturday so that she and Sal could discuss it."

"Should we?" said Eli with an amused smile as you looked at Sal who smiled back. "We'll see."

For the almost three years that Eli had gotten to know Sal, they never talked about personal relationships, although they did share stories about their family backgrounds. Conversations were always about the news of the day, local events, family stories, and, of course, flowers. Eli had wondered whether or not Sal was straight or gay or whatever. She was initially concerned about why an adult man would befriend a young boy, but, once a few months had passed, she came to understand that Sal was simply a kind person who grew up in a stable, loving family. Sal had encouraged Wilbur to become a better observer of the natural world and helped Wilbur to keep journals in which he wrote detailed descriptions of each rock he collected. Because Wilbur had a very infrequent and cool relationship with his own father, Eli saw Sal as being a strong role model for Wilbur. She was also impressed with the philosophical nature of the conversations between Sal and Wilbur. As Wilbur approached puberty with his body changing and his voice becoming raspy, it was Sal who was able to broach the subject with Wilbur without any embarrassment or reluctance on Wilbur's part. Eli was grateful for Sal being in Wilbur's life.

Eli dared to ask, "Sal, would it be okay with you if we invited Sally to breakfast next Saturday. I don't want to put you in a difficult position. You know, I've never asked if you are in a relationship or prefer not to be."

"Eli, I get the impression that Wilbur is trying to set me up."

"Well…"

"It's okay. I'm not in a relationship at the moment. In fact, it's been a while. And I don't mind being set up. My mother tries it all the time. I'm not really very good at meeting women."

Eli laughed and thought if only Sal knew how difficult it was for her to meet other men. She often thought that she must put off some kind of chemical warning, "Don't approach; I'm not available." She understood exactly what Sal meant.

After the "set-up" breakfast and after Sal left, Eli asked Sally what she thought of Sal. Wilbur sat quietly at the patio table with the delight of being a matchmaker.

"Not my type," said Sally. "He's very nice, but not my type."

Wilbur interjected, "He's really a good guy."

"I'm sure he is, Wilbur, but he's too quiet and seems directionless."

Nothing more was said, or perhaps Wilbur just stopped listening as his mother and Sally continued to talk. The next day, when he and Sal were out collecting, Wilbur told Sal that Sally didn't seem interested. "She said you're not her type and that you lack direction."

"Finding the right person isn't easy. My parents found each other early in their lives. Unfortunately, your mom and dad were not a good match, but it doesn't make either of them bad people. It's really okay, Wilbur." Sal put his hand on Wilbur's shoulder, gave it a squeeze, and said, "Thanks for the attempted set-up, Wilbur. Maybe next time."

Sally loved watermelon, but she didn't do a good job of selecting them. She was strolling through the mid-week Bear City farmer's market when she came to a stand with a large supply of melons. She asked the vendor to pick out a good watermelon for her when she heard Sal's voice behind her, "Let me help. I'm really good at this."

Sally turned and there was Sal smiling and offering his assistance. He pulled a melon from the pile in front of them, hefted it in his hands to test its weight. "It should feel heavy for its size," said Sal. "And let's look for the yellow spot where it rested on the ground. It should look creamy yellow. Okay, there it is. Now I'll give it a thump and listen for a good deep sound. That will tell us if it's a good juicy one. Yep, this is the one you'll want."

"So, you are not only a flower collector but also a watermelon man."

"Wilbur calls me a Flower Bandit, but I like to think of myself as a man with a few other talents. Not too many to make me arrogant, but, like a watermelon, just right in the moment. Apparently, I'm not everybody's type, though."

Sally blushed just a tad and looked at Sal with a bit of a crooked smile. "Well, thank you, Sal. I appreciate the help."

"I'm sorry. I shouldn't have said that. It was a feeble attempt at humor and completely inappropriate. How about if I make it up to you by buying you coffee?"

"Well, I really can't turn down a coffee apology."

They walked over to Pop's Donuts and Coffee where Sal ordered a black coffee and old-fashioned donut and Sally an iced tea. "I can't drink coffee this late in the day," she explained.

Sal said, "I really am sorry. I'm not very skilled at always saying the right things. Sometimes I can be flip and then instantly regret it."

Sally said she understood and sometimes she could be just as unthinking. They spoke for over an hour over refills of coffee and iced tea with Sally's watermelon keeping her company in the booth while Sal sat across from her. Phyllis, who owned the café with her husband Jack, remarked to Jack that it was nice to see Sal not sitting alone for a change.

He was a regular customer, but never with anyone. "Jack, It looks like Sal might be on a date. I've never seen him with anyone."

Sally asked Sal how he had become known as the Flower Bandit. He explained the time he and Wilbur first met and when Wilbur called him the Flower Bandit.

"It just stuck. And Wilbur became the Stone Bandit. But his nickname didn't really stick with him."

"The two of you are really quite a pair," said Sally. "Wilbur's mother is grateful for you being such a good adult in his life. Why the daily flower picking?"

Sal explained that it had to do with his philosophy of beauty. He believed starting each day with a joyful thought and a search for beauty was a key to happiness. Sally asked if he had grown up in a religious family that practiced those kinds of rituals.

"No, my family was not religious at all. And I'm not either. However, I do find meaning in nature, especially flowers. I've developed my own routines without any expectation for others to agree or disagree with them."

"You sound like you might be a practicing pagan."

"Far from it," said Sal. "If anything, I'm totally anti-religion. I do find a certain spiritual connection to nature, but not from any kind of religious view. No, it's just a personal sense of things. I find comfort in beauty and joy."

Sally did not expect their conversation to go so deep into personal beliefs. She thought she had just agreed to a coffee apology, but she was enjoying the moment. She shared that she had grown up in a secular Jewish family, where they enjoyed the holidays and traditions without any forced belief in god.

"We weren't told to be agnostic or atheist. We were only expected to form our own beliefs. I think my entire belief system revolves around the food. My grandmother's knishes and kugel cannot be beat," she said with the brightest smile of the day and a look in her eye that invited more conversation.

They agreed to meet for coffee again at the following week's farmer's market; that meeting turned into another and then dinner and then many more dinners.

Over several months, Sally talked about her art and her search for beauty through watercolors. She shared her early days as a middle school art teacher and how she loved working with that age group but couldn't tolerate a school setting.

"It was too confining for me. Schedules and meetings and so many rules. The tension between the union and the administration was palpable. I just wanted to be left alone to teach art. I didn't have the temperament to be a good employee. When my work began to sell, I was able to afford my independence. Teaching wasn't for me, but I really admire those who do that really difficult and important work. And kids need art teachers who can feel more satisfaction in that setting. I couldn't."

"That's why I work at home," said Sal. "I also have difficulty working in a traditional work setting. I think we have an awful lot in common."

Sal and Sally had been seeing each other for almost six months. Most of their time was spent at Pop's and Phyllis and Jack were convinced that they were "an item." Other than coffee, iced tea and an occasional donut for Sal and a number of casual dinners at local restaurants, there wasn't much romance or physical intimacy between the two. Their time together usually ended with a hug and a light kiss, but nothing more. They appeared to be content with each other's company and conversation.

Sally was delivering another watercolor when Eli brought up Sal. They were seated on the living room sofa when Eli said, "I understand you and Sal are seeing each other pretty regularly. How's it going with him?"

"He's a really great guy."

"Is there something more there?" asked Eli.

"I don't know," said Sally. "I'm not sure he's my type."

Wilbur had been off to the side listening intently to the conversation. He was feeling bewildered and couldn't believe that Sally didn't see Sal as her type. Had nothing changed since they first met? Sal had shared with Wilbur his affection for Sally, and Wilbur thought they perhaps he had been a successful matchmaker.

"How can you say that?" implored Wilbur. "What do you mean 'not my type'? What is your type?"

"Wilbur, that's not appropriate!" exclaimed his mother. She had never heard Wilbur be so impolite. "You have no right to say such things. Now apologize."

"It's okay, Eli. I know Wilbur just cares."

"I do care," said Wilbur. "I care about you and Sal. You've been spending a lot of time together. I thought the two of you might be together for a long time. What is your type?"

Sally invited Wilbur to sit on the chair across from the sofa she and Eli were sitting on. With a calm and empathetic voice, she said, "I know you'd like us to be a couple, but we're really just friends. When I say I'm not sure he's my type, I'm saying that there doesn't seem to be a chemistry between us. Do you know what I mean?"

Wilbur was quiet, looked down at his bare feet before he made eye contact with Sally and blurting out, "If you want chemistry try going into a lab. I mean chemistry is just an excuse for staying apart. I know you like Sal and I know Sal likes you. I can tell when I see you together. Hey, sometimes chemistry comes later…after friendship…after trust…after time!"

The stillness that followed Wilbur's outburst filled the space between the three of them. Eli was nonplussed by her son's unusual behavior. Wilbur began to fidget a bit and started to stand. He felt embarrassed and out of place.

"Please, stay there a moment, Wilbur. I'm thankful for how much you care."

Wilbur never said anything to Sal about his outburst, and neither did Eli. At the next farmer's market, Sal was standing at the melon stand when Sally remarked, "I know something about picking out a good watermelon. This guy showed me once, and I've never been the same."

Sal turned and said, "Oh, really?"

"Yeah, it's remarkable how the talent of selecting a good melon can rub off on others. And it's remarkable how wise a young Wilbur can be. There's this whole philosophy about chemistry and types I never knew anything about. Maybe you'd like to talk about it over at Pop's?"

A Good Melon is Hard to Find

The garden was lush with bursts of colorful flowers. A recently constructed arbor in the far corner teemed with climbing sweet pea and clematis. The lawn's perimeter was randomly filled with many varieties and colors of roses, poppies, daisies, marigolds, and other annual and perennial plants. The garden was scented like a dozen expensive perfumes. When Eli asked Sal to add color to the formerly bland space, her only request was to keep it full of "serendipitous surprise." Wilbur helped with the planting and with the strategic placement of rocks and some purchased boulders. His collected pile of stones, large rocks almost big enough to be called small boulders, and castoff concrete still remained but was seen more as an idiosyncratic accumulation rather than an eyesore. Tucked into a corner of the yard were a pair of watermelon vines, an ironic reminder of the circumstances when Sal and Sally first met and when Sally first realized that Sal was her type, or, at least, close to her type.

Wilbur was about to turn thirteen. He was now as tall as Sal and almost as lanky. He wore his hair long and shaggy like Sal's and his voice had become deeper and more authoritative. He rarely saw his biological father; Sal had become his best friend and adult mentor. They still walked most mornings with Sal looking for flowers and Wilbur for unusual rocks. However, the last year had produced big changes with Sal's and Sally's engagement. Their upcoming wedding ceremony would take place in Eli's garden.

When Eli insisted that the ceremony be held in her backyard, she also offered to take care of all the essentials, including the food and wedding cake. This was to be the first marriage for both Sal and Sally, and they were in their early forties and not interested in a big hoopla. Sal's parents were still alive, but Sally's were not. Neither had any siblings, only a few aunts and uncles and distant cousins. Their circle of friends was small and intimate. They thought the wedding might include around fifteen to twenty folks. They happily accepted Eli's offer of the yard for the wedding venue but insisted on hiring a caterer to take care of the food and the wedding cake. After a number of Eli's breakfasts and casual lunches, Sal reminded Sally that a meal of packaged and prepared food was not a good idea. They had already experienced a series of breakfast toaster treats, canned meats, deli case salads, flavored bottled ice teas, and gooey store-bought baked goods. Sal could only imagine what Eli might serve at a wedding if given the opportunity. He and Sally were not gourmands, as evidenced by their many dates at Pop's Donut and Coffee where Phyllis kept their drinks filled and served an occasional plain old-fashioned donut to Sal before keeping watch behind the counter and filling in her husband Jack about the growing Sal and Sally relationship.

When Sal and Sally informed Phyllis and Jack of their upcoming nuptials, Phyllis immediately offered to cater the event. She explained that Jack was a culinary institute graduate. "Even though we run a donut and coffee shop, Jack is a really good chef. This little café gives us economic stability and some independence from having employees and all the headaches that entails. But, when we're at home, Jack cooks up a storm worthy of any fine restaurant. Let us create a menu for you and you can try some samples."

A few weeks later, Sal and Sally sat at the café's counter after closing hours sampling some of the most delectable food they had ever tasted. Phyllis explained that Jack had created a menu for a casual meal. They tasted appetizers that included miniature crab cakes, a watermelon, mint and feta salad in tribute of Sal and Sally's melon story, and vegetarian gazpacho. Dinner options included pulled pork sliders, shrimp kebabs, and a vegetable risotto. Sally said that carrot cake was her favorite, which Jack said he could make with and without walnuts. He also said that a fruity sorbet would be nice for those who wanted something lighter.

"There won't be many at the wedding and we don't need a ton of food," said Sally.

"Since it's a backyard wedding and reception, we'll set everything up under a tent and serve buffet style. Jack and I can handle the service. This will allow us to be there for the wedding. We don't want to miss it," said Phyllis.

As the final few months before the wedding approached, Sal, Sally, Eli and Wilbur gathered in Eli's backyard to talk about last minute details. Sally had brought a package wrapped in brown Kraft paper and handed it to Eli. She explained that she was so thankful for all that Eli had already done and wanted her to have a special thank-you gift. Eli carefully folded back the paper wrapping to find a watercolor rendering of the backyard's arbor and surrounding color. Inside the arbor was a depiction of several watermelons.

Eli said, "It's beautiful, Sally. And you've put watermelons under the arbor."

"I think Sal and I are a couple because of the melon stand at the farmer's market. I guess a good melon is hard to find. But I've found mine," said Sally.

Eli described the perfect spot for hanging the new painting before Sal talked about the wedding party. The invited guests had grown to almost thirty. Sal and Sally hadn't realized that their circle of friends was larger than they thought, especially after word got out that they were engaged. They decided that Sal's father would officiate the ceremony. Sally had already asked Eli to be her maid of honor and that there would be no other members of the wedding party.

Wilbur asked, "Who's going to be your best man?"

"Well, you Wilbur. You're going to be my best man and ring bearer."

Everything seemed to be in place. Wilbur felt so proud of his important role, and he wanted to do something special for Sal and Sally. He asked his mother for advice, but she had no suggestions other than to be himself and enjoy the moment. The wedding was scheduled for the last Saturday in the month, a day Wilbur was supposed to be with his father. It wasn't a hard and fast rule, as Wilbur often missed that time because of other conflicts. Often those conflicts were activities his father had with his second family. Wilbur's father had remarried a few years after his divorce from Eli. He and Wilbur's stepmother had two children of their own and Wilbur didn't feel connected to what he called "a second chance family." His connection to his father was more of an obligation and the time spent together was always tense and distant. His father was a wealthy person who continued to provide financial support to Eli and Wilbur with few strings attached. He did possess a demanding personality under a veneer of pleasantness. When he was informed about Sal and Sally's wedding and Wilbur's role in it, he suggested the date ought to be changed because it was his weekend to have Wilbur. Having things and people were important to Wilbur's father.

After several phone calls, characterized by forced politeness, between Eli and her ex-husband, it was agreed to have everyone meet and try to work out an agreeable solution. Wilbur never referred to his father by name. When Eli told him of the meeting, Wilbur said he would have nothing to do with it.

"It's his way of controlling me. I'm done with him," proclaimed Wilbur. "He can't force us to change the wedding date. It's not going to happen."

Eli explained that there were certain parental rights that needed to be followed. She told Wilbur that his father could withhold other support as a consequence if they didn't adhere to the terms of the divorce. Wilbur likened it to legal blackmail. Once he calmed down, he returned to his usual too-mature-for-his-age temperament and agreed that there should be a meeting to iron out the conflict.

Wilbur's father rang the doorbell and then knocked several times before Eli opened the front door. He filled the door. A huge man wearing a red baseball cap on a head of dark, unruly hair. His unibrow was bushy and untrimmed. His face pockmarked and menacing. He sported a holstered pistol on a belt featuring an oversized silver buckle in the shape of a bald eagle. Eli waved him in and remarked that it was a gun-free home. Her former husband said he needed it for protection. He claimed that he was an easy target for abduction and ransom demands. Wilbur's father ran a huge and profitable hedge fund. Their divorce settlement provided Eli and Wilbur with a very comfortable life. Other than Wilbur's required monthly visits with his father, there were no other conditions.

Wilbur's father asked where Wilbur was and Eli replied that he, Sal and Sally were outside on the patio. "I'd like to avoid conflict. Let's go into the library where we can discuss a proposal I have for you." They entered a small room with bookshelves lining two walls, a modern glass-topped desk stood in front of a draped window with two wingback chairs facing the desk. The room was painted a creamy white, which gave the illusion that the books were floating in mid-air. Eli was a reader and she had read all of the books that filled those shelves.

Eli pointed to her ex-husband and asked him to have a seat while she sat across from him on her ergonomic desk chair. Eli stopped referring to her ex-husband by name immediately after their divorce. He was "your father", "the man who fathered my child", "the guy that affords me a lifestyle", "my ex", and even "he who shall go nameless." They had virtually no contact. Even on those weekends when she drove the few miles to his walled estate sitting on hundreds of acres of pristine countryside just outside the city, she dropped Wilbur off at the entrance of the four-story mansion and drove away after watching him enter through the enormous, hand-carved doors that seemed to say, "Welcome, and be careful."

Eli took a quiet breath while holding a confident stare at the beast of a man seated across from her. At one time, he was not such an imposing figure. He was tall and fit when they were first married. He was just beginning a career as a financial manager before establishing a hedge fund that brought them unimaginable wealth. With that wealth came his size, paranoia, and abusive behavior. After Wilbur was born, he became distant and illusive. When she discovered his illicit relationships and questionable financial dealings, she created a damaging portfolio she used to secure her divorce.

He asked, "What do you want?"

She began, "I have a proposal for you. You and I both know that you are using Wilbur to hurt me. We need to put an end to the hurt. And you know I have items in my safe that you'd like to have. Here's a document I want you to sign. If you do, we're done. Wilbur will choose if and when he wants to see you. I have a feeling it may take some time, but he will eventually want to reconnect. But not now. Sign this paper and we can go on with our lives without either of us holding something over one another. I had my attorney draw it up. It's legal."

Wilbur's father read over the paper, pulled his cell phone out of his pocket, and called his attorney. There was a perfunctory discussion before he ended the call and asked if he would be getting the originals. Eli said he would. He said any copies she kept would be inadmissible in any future legal action. He signed the document and called his banker giving instructions for the immediate transfer of funds to Eli's bank account. After Eli confirmed the transfer, she reached into a desk drawer and pulled out a large manila folder, which she handed to her ex-husband.

"Eli, you and Wilbur won't have to ever worry about future finances. Please, tell him I hope he'll call me soon." He stood and left.

Eli was relieved when her ex strode off. She often asked herself why she had ever married him and could only answer that it was her own immaturity, anxiousness to get away from her own dysfunctional family, and find comfort in being cared for. She soon realized that sacrificing her identity to a bully had trapped her into unhappiness. Her perspective on her own life and motherhood changed everything. After giving birth to Wilbur, it took her five years to gather the incriminating evidence of her husband's private malfeasance and infidelity, and then to confront and finally divorce him. Now, she had taken action one step further, and essentially divorced him from Wilbur. And she found it remarkably easy to accomplish once she fully realized that her ex's narcissism made it easy to negotiate what she wanted. Eli would tell Wilbur that he was no longer required to spend one weekend each month with his father; rather, he could now choose when he would see him.

Sal, Sally and Wilbur were in animated conversation when Eli walked out to the patio. They turned and saw she was alone. Wilbur asked, "Where's dad?" Eli explained that he was no longer an impediment to the wedding plans, and it was no longer necessary to meet with him.

"Let's get on with some last-minute arrangements," stated Eli. "I know you have Phyllis and Jack catering, but I still want to offer something. Yes, I know not to use any packaged food," she said while laughing. "However, I'd like to make a big, fresh fruit salad. What melons would you like me to include?"

Deconstructing Elizabeth Ruth

When Eli was a young girl, she learned to live in solitude and enjoy arithmetic. She spent many hours alone in her bedroom and away from her constantly arguing parents. When not reading books, checked out from the adult library, not the children's or young adult's sections, she invented a game using her extensive doll collection as the players. She engaged her dolls in elaborate baseball games using a pair of dice to determine hits, outs, and other game actions. She kept detailed statistics for each of her players. In the beginning, she used simple arithmetic to keep track of how well her players did, but, as she learned how to calculate percentages and batting averages, her data became more sophisticated. By the time she entered high school and ended her imaginative play, she had accumulated almost ten binders filled with player's statistical histories. It wasn't surprising that she became something of a high school math nerd and was called upon to be the official scorekeeper and statistician for all of her school's major sports, except when she competed on the track team.

In spite of spending so much time in her room alone and in solitary play, Eli made friends easily. She was always the tallest girl in her elementary school classes, which usually meant being one of the tallest students in her age group. Of course, that changed when boys reached puberty and their growth spurts pushed them taller than the girls. She used her height to her advantage. When seeing a bully trying to intimidate another girl, she casually walked over to the victim and stood silent and tall with her arms crossed. That usually put an end to the confrontation. Eli found that size and silence was often the best cure for a tense situation. She was a master of the stare down. Should the bully not immediately back down or even appear to be aggressive toward Eli, she would take one confident stride toward him or her while dropping her arms to her side and smiling ever so faintly. That always did the trick. And she also had the benefit of making a new friend. Eli had quite a few friends in elementary school. None were ever invited over to her home to play. Her friendships remained at school.

She reached her full height in seventh grade and early adolescence had transformed her into a slender, pretty young woman who loved school and despised home life. She began taking care of the way she looked and dressed. Eli developed a reputation as a reliable and trustworthy babysitter. It was another way to be out of her house while earning spending money, which she saved and would use to regularly treat herself to a stylish hairdo. Her parents had the means to afford her nice clothes and an occasional treat, but rarely gave her any attention. She was given a modest weekly allowance along with lunch money with the admonition to "make it last." Her parents were not aware that her babysitting money afforded her many more options than most of her peers. Eli was fine with her growing independence and learned more about life from her voracious reading than from her parents. She developed a strong moral core, which kept her from adolescent foolishness. She demurred from junior high school social events, and, even in high school when boys were frequently asking her out to a movie or party, she usually declined. The few dates she went on were with groups of friends and mostly outdoor activities like picnics or hikes in the countryside. Her first kiss was after the junior prom, a date she accepted much to her best friend's surprise. In her high school freshman year, she made a personal commitment that she would leave home and go off a to college many miles away. She used a compass to draw a three-hundred-mile radius from her home and identified all the colleges to which she might apply. Her PSAT scores were a guarantee of a full academic scholarship to a good school. She felt that she was lining up her life for success.

She met her best friend in the sixth grade. Lori had reached puberty early and the boys referred to her as the "girl with boobs." One morning before school, three boys had surrounded her on the playground and were verbally taunting her. Eli approached with her well-established, quiet confidence and stood across from the boy who looked to be the leader.

"What are you looking at, Eli?"

No other words were spoken. There were only a few elongated seconds of silence before the three boys walked away. From that point on, Lori and Eli were inseparable at school. They were able to share whatever young adolescent girls needed to share about their changing bodies and the uncertainty that came with a different kind of attention. When Eli reached puberty in the seventh grade, it was Lori and Lori's mother Mrs. Abraham who helped her to understand and celebrate the change she was going through. It was Lori who accompanied her to the store to buy her first package of menstrual pads and she and her mother who talked to her about how to use them. Eli eventually struck up the courage to inform her mother that she had reached womanhood and her mother replied, "Welcome to the curse. Now, don't get pregnant." After her father heard about her leap into maturity, his response was with a typically crude, sarcastic and unoriginal sexist adage, "Now you've got what all the boys want, so don't get pregnant. You know what they say, 'old enough to bleed; old enough to butcher.'"

Those were the last words Eli had with her parents about growing up. In fact, they were pretty much the last words she had with them at all. From then on, her practice of familial avoidance rose to artistic heights. And they didn't seem to notice. She never again sought their advice, nor did she offer them any information about her growing private life. Eli was comforted by Lori's mother after she related how her parents had reacted. Mrs. Abraham, a large, fleshy woman, quietly listened as Eli tearfully told a story of her insensitive and uncaring parents who were constantly arguing. Mrs. Abraham pulled Eli into an almost smothering bear hug and told her that she had another home whenever she needed it.

Eli and Lori became even closer friends. Shortly, after what became known between them as the "playground incident", they both vowed to never allow a boy to intimidate them. Little did they know how things would change as they grew older and began to seek approval from others. Little did they know that when Eli went off to college to study mathematics and physics, she would meet her future ex-husband Sid. Little did they know that Sid would convince Eli to change her major to business with the goal of making money and finding financial independence. Little did they know that Eli would endure her own unhappy and destructive ten-year marriage before finally achieving safety and security with her then five-year old son Wilbur.

Eli and Lori began to dress like twin sisters. They both entered young adulthood as attractive young women in their own unique way. Eli had a model's stereotypical body, long and lithesome. She walked with an easy, confident glide. Lori was more like her mother. She was medium height with a softness that bordered on pudgy. Over time, she learned to walk with purpose and excellent posture. They couldn't share clothes, but they did enjoy purchasing matching outfits and allowing them to plan matching school outfits. Others began calling them the "Ello" twins by combining Eli and Lori, which they took as a compliment. They were both outstanding students. In Eli's junior year, she began taking advanced math classes at the local community college after she had mastered every advanced placement class offered at the high school. Lori was something of a science whiz and immersed herself in biological sciences. This would ultimately serve her well when she went off to university to prepare for medical school and eventually become a pediatrician back in Bear City. Although Eli and Lori went to different colleges, they maintained their close friendship through lengthy phone calls, and both eventually returned to their hometown. Unfortunately, Eli returned with a husband and an unhappy marriage.

When they weren't studying, they ran track. Eli gave the appearance of always being in motion, except for those times when she used her quiet stare down to put an end to conflict. She had long runner's legs and excelled at cross country and middle-distance races during track season. She preferred a plain track outfit with white athletic socks and white track shoes. Lori didn't look like a sprinter, but she was amazingly fast, and she sported an explosion of loud colors right down to her fluorescent orange track shoes.

They both became coffee drinkers in their senior year. Pop's Donuts and Coffee was where high school students hung out after school and on weekends. Proprietors Wendy and Dooley "Pops" Jones enjoyed the teenage energy that filled the coffee shop each weekday afternoon. They had only one hard and fast rule: "no profanity." Pop's offered more than just coffee and donuts; the menu also listed a variety of breakfast and lunch items. Dooley's chili had achieved legendary status among the citizens of Bear City. Every morning after preparing dozens of fresh donuts, Dooley set about cooking a huge pot of chili, which could be bought by the bowl or used to smother omelets, hamburgers, hotdogs or anything else that might be requested. Dooley would often say, "Slop my chili on anything your stomach or heart desires."

Eli and Lori would sit at a window booth several times each week nursing heavily creamed and sugared coffees and talk about their current and future lives. Lori's family was large and boisterous. She was the youngest sibling with four older brothers. Her father was Bear City's busiest and most respected family practitioner. Two of her older brothers were already doctors living in other parts of the country, one was still in medical school and the youngest brother a sophomore in college. Mrs. Abraham was a stay-at-home wife and mother, who enjoyed her role while encouraging Lori to find her own path in life free from how others might try to define her. Lori felt no pressure to become a doctor; rather, she relished the thought of going into what her brothers called the "family business."

Eli often asked, "Don't you feel the pressure of expectation?"

"Not really. My parents have only asked that I do my best and pursue what will make me happy. I see how happy my family is and hope to have the same."

"But your mother isn't a doctor."

Lori said, "She says it never occurred to her. She once thought of being an actor. She was a drama major in college and appeared in a lot of plays. She still gets a part once in a while in the community theater, but she always says her happiness is being a mother."

"I'm jealous. My parents are so horrible. I could never imagine being trapped in such a relationship. I want to go to college and become a mathematician or a physicist."

Once their conversation turned to religion. Lori said her family was loosely Jewish. "Abraham, after all. But we don't really practice. In fact, I think my father is an atheist."

"And you?" asked Eli.

"Oh, I'm not sure. I really don't think about it. My two oldest brothers had bar mitzvahs. My two youngest couldn't bother. My father never talks about his, but I know he had one. We never go to temple, but we sort of pay attention to some of the holidays if my grandparents invite us. And that's not very often. What about you, Eli?"

Eli looked a little bemused by the question. There was no form or expression of religion in her home. She hadn't thought much about it and her reply caused Lori to laugh. "I think I'd be either Jewish or Rastafarian. But then I'd have to choose between bad wine or weed, and I'm not really interested in smoking joints or drinking horribly sweet wine. I suppose I'll have to see what happens."

Eli was accepted by her first-choice university, and granted a full scholarship including living expenses. She informed Lori and Mrs. Abraham and was immediately invited to stay for a celebratory dinner.

"I know you can't wait to move out of your home; still, your parents must be very proud," stated Mrs. Abraham.

Eli, Lori and Lori's parents were seated at the dining room table. Dr. Abraham had a very successful medical practice and finances were never an issue. They could have lived much more lavish lives, but they owned a modest home furnished in a lot of family hand-me-down furniture. They took annual family vacations to the same mountain cabin that had been in the family for generations. All of their children were required to work for their allowances by doing household chores. Lori, like Eli, also earned extra spending money by babysitting. Eli had very much become part of their family. She frequently stayed overnight and had been given use of one of the extra bedrooms now that the brothers were no longer at home.

"I haven't told my parents. I'm not sure I will. It's hard to believe, but things at home have gotten even stranger. My parents don't really argue that much anymore, but the hostility is still there. They've gotten eerily silent. And we don't really talk anymore. We haven't for a couple of years, and I'm fine with it," replied Eli. "You and Doctor Abraham are more like my real parents."

Doctor Abraham, who was usually very quiet listened intently. He looked across the table at Mrs. Abraham and said, "Eli always has a place at our table." And turning to Eli, "We are very proud of you. I am so sad that you feel our home is your real home, but we will always be here for you. You are loved here."

Eli's eyes filled with tears and with trembling lips said, "I know. And I love you, too."

Lori stood and went around the table to give Eli a hug. "You are my sister."

It's difficult to understand why some families are so loving and others so hate-filled. In Eli's family there were generations of dysfunction without hardly any divorces. It seemed that her family history was a history of bickering bitterness. It was as though her lineage thrived on conflict. Eli, however, had emerged from it seemingly unscathed. She discovered quiet reflection as a relief from what she felt was the terror of her household. By the time she was in high school, she had developed a lasting resilience to the mayhem of her home life. She was no longer surprised by her bizarre family situation. She had essentially divorced herself from her family without seeking formal emancipation. Her parents didn't even seem to notice.

The morning after her college acceptance celebratory dinner with Lori and Lori's parents, which she felt was her real family, she went to her own house to retrieve some clothes and other essential items. She hadn't been back for several weeks and, when she arrived, found the house empty and an envelope taped to the front door addressed to "Elizabeth Ruth."

She read the short note with some relief. After gathering much more of what she had come for, she called Lori and asked if she and her mother could come and pick her up. They arrived shortly, helped her load clothes, books, and a couple of boxes filled with books and a variety of sentimental items, which included one binder full of one season's statistics for her invented baseball games.

Before driving over to pick up Eli, Mrs. Abraham had called her husband and asked if he could break away from the clinic and meet them back at their house. They gathered in the living room. Mrs. Abraham explained that Eli's parents had left Bear City without saying where they had gone. The short note they left informed Eli that she was free to live her own life and that she should contact a Mr. Masterson, an attorney who would manage a small trust they had set up to help Eli through the remainder of high school and the first four years of college. Her parents didn't know she had already secured a scholarship.

Doctor Abraham called Mr. Masterson and was informed that Eli's parents had signed several documents that formally liberated Elizabeth Ruth. Mr. Masterson had also been given authority to dispose of their house and any other property left behind that Eli did not want. The sale of the home and other items would be used to fund Eli's small trust.

Eli remained stoically calm upon hearing the details of her formal abandonment. Lori sat on the sofa with her arm around Eli's shoulder and her eyes watering. When Doctor Abraham finished explaining everything to Eli, he said, "I can't imagine the hurt you must be feeling. What a cruel thing your parents have done. You are welcome to stay with us as long as you want. You are part of our family."

"My parents named me Elizabeth Ruth, but I have never been her. My name is Eli. And it's good to finally be home."

Wilbur and Sam

Wilbur had finally decided to give up being an architect and began working full-time as a builder of stone walls. Turning thirty was on the horizon and he was feeling a different purpose for his life. He made the conscious decision that he didn't want to merely imagine, with architectural design and speculation, what might be; rather, he wanted to construct, with his bare hands, tangible structures that grew organically and harmoniously from its landscape. He sought to merge creativity and actuality.

Wilbur's passion was selecting, lifting, and fitting stones together to build a wall that defined and gave purpose to its surrounding space. The work required strength and precision and Wilbur's body had become tautly muscled with the hours upon hours of rigorous work. He was standing in front of the wall he was constructing across the front of the Burnside's property, which was adjacent to Bear City Middle School. It was a warm day; Wilbur had taken off his T-shirt and stood tanned and bare-chested while he studied the progress he was making.

Samantha, one of the school's science teachers, walked by and remarked, "Beautiful wall. I've seen you working on it for the last couple of days. Are you doing it all by yourself?"

Holding a large tote bag filled a few books and student science journals, Samantha appeared to be about Wilbur's age. In some ways, she reminded Wilbur of his mother with her tall, lean stature, short hair, and piercing green eyes. Her skin was flawless and the only makeup she wore was pale pink lipstick that was more of a translucent lip gloss than a bold color popular by many trendy, young women. She appeared to be comfortable and self-assured.

Wilbur felt a little self-conscious standing shirtless. He bent over, picked up his T-shirt and slipped it on before responding, "Thanks. I think it's coming along. I'm trying to figure out how to make the turn back to the corner of the house. It needs to flow back naturally and follow the contour of the lot."

"You're really putting a lot of thought into a wall. Are you building a wall or creating an art project?"

"It's a little of both."

Wilbur and Samantha continued talking about the wall with Wilbur explaining that he never draws plans before beginning the project. Instead, he and his client talk about what they are hoping to achieve and then leave it up to Wilbur to "make it happen." There are no contracts other than an agreement about cost and an estimated time for completing the work. Wilbur uses rocks gathered from a large swathe of land bordering the Bear River. The acreage along the river belongs to his mother's best friend and possesses several acres of river rock easily accessed and gathered.

"My interest in rocks began as a child. And then I met my friend Sal who liked collecting flowers."

Samantha asked, "Could I try placing a rock?"

"Well, this next one is pretty heavy, but you can give it a try." Wilbur showed Samantha the large rock, really a small boulder, and where to place it. "Use your knees to lift and settle it gently right here," as Wilbur pointed to the intended location.

Samantha bent over and was immediately stopped my Wilbur. "Don't bend. Do more of a squat and lift with your legs. Let me show you." Wilbur lifted the stone and set it back in place.

"Okay, I'll try." Samantha hefted the heavy stone just as Wilbur instructed, but, before she could move it into place, dropped it just missing her right foot as she jumped back.

"Geez! That was close. I don't think I'll try it again."

"Are you okay?" Wilbur stooped to check on Samantha's foot. "Did that get you?"

"I'm fine. It was close."

"Let me make it up to you. I shouldn't have let you try to pick up such a heavy one."

Wilbur said it was time for him to take a break and asked Samantha if she'd like to get a drink and a snack at Pop's Donut's and Coffee. They ended up riding over to Pop's in Wilbur's partially restored 1947 Ford one-ton flatbed pick-up truck. He had done all the work himself and had yet to get into the interior. The bench seat needed reupholstering. The speedometer was accurate up to 30 miles per hour, the gas gauge never moved from full, and the decrepit dashboard was in need of replacement. Wilbur had replaced the old engine with a modern motor, and he had completely rebuilt the suspension and brake systems. The truck was safe, although few invited riders accepted rides. Samantha had no issue with sitting on torn upholstery. And she laughed when the window simply dropped into the door when she tried winding it down.

"I'm still working on the restoration," said Wilbur.

When they walked into Pop's, Sal was seated at the booth that Wilbur and Sal frequented on almost a daily basis. Wilbur and Sal had been friends for twenty years. They began as flower and rock collectors, which, from time to time, they still did. Sal works part time from home as a customer service representative for an online retailer. He has also developed a successful business selling signed prints of the flower pictures he had accumulated over the last twenty years. His wife Sally, to whom Wilbur's mother Eli introduced, is a successful watercolor artist, and she and Sal often set up a booth at art fairs around the state. Sal sat nursing a latte and a jelly donut. With all the donuts he has consumed over the years, he is fortunate enough to remain trim. The only indications he has grown older are streaks of gray in his long hair and a few crow's feet around his curious eyes.

"Sal, I've brought along a new friend. Actually, an almost broken-footed friend," Wilbur said jokingly.

"Hi, Sal. I'm Sam."

"Well, now I finally know your name," added Wilbur. As it dawned on him that he had yet to introduce himself.

"That's true. Nice to meet you," said Samantha holding out her hand to shake Wilbur's. "I'm Samantha, but I go by Sam. And you are?" All of this said with a smile and a quiet nod to Sal."

Wilbur calmly shook Samantha's hand and answered, "I'm Wilbur. And from now on you're Sam." They slid into the booth across from Sal as Phyllis, who owned Pop's with her husband Jack, arrived to take their orders. Wilbur asked what Sam would like and she requested an iced tea. Wilbur ordered a black coffee and an old-fashioned donut.

Wilbur explained how Sam had dropped a large rock that almost landed on her foot, and that he felt obligated to make up for his negligence in allowing the almost catastrophe. Sal listened with a smile, nodding toward Sam in the same quiet way she had nodded to him.

Turning to Sam he asked, "Did Wilbur drive you over in that thing he calls a restored truck?"

"Well, I'm a science teacher at the middle school. Perhaps, I should have run some forensic tests on the interior, but I think I'll live."

Wilbur was even more attracted to Sam's sense of humor, notwithstanding her profile, curiosity and green eyes. Wilbur did not currently have a girlfriend. He had been in a couple of serious relationships, but none had what his mother Eli referred to as "long term possibilities." The women in his life were all very nice. Wilbur had a way of dating intelligent, self-assured, independent women. He was very much a product of his mother's independent feminism. He had been raised to be keenly aware of the inequalities and injustices that existed everywhere, even in Bear City.

His mother insisted that he become involved in high school community service projects. His commitment to social justice issues lasted throughout college. Now, he stayed actively involved in several local community organizations involved with outreach to the homeless population and with progressive political causes. He had yet to meet a woman who shared his commitment to social issues. He wondered if Sam might be different.

"My wife Sally once taught art at the middle school. I'm sure it was years before you began there. Teaching just wasn't for her."

"It can be really hard," said Sam, "but I really enjoy the kids, especially their energy. It's a bit like teaching hormones who wear tennis shoes." Wilbur and Sam laughed. "You can't teach middle school without a sense of humor."

The three of them talked for about thirty minutes before Sam said she needed to get home. She explained that she had a stack of science journals to grade and wanted to finish before dinner. Wilbur asked if he could take her to dinner. Sam said, "I'd like that. How about 7:00?" She wrote her address and phone number on a napkin before Wilbur drove her back to his wall construction site.

Wilbur drove home looking forward to his date with Sam. Eli was in the backyard sitting at the glass-topped patio table with her closest friend Lori, drinking lemonade, and enjoying the view of her yard filled with a variety of colorful flowers. The arbor, which was used for Sal's and Sally's wedding ceremony, was now covered with red, yellow and white climbing roses. The spot where Wilbur had once piled his collection of rocks, broken concrete, and other interesting stones, was now a kitchen garden filled with herbs, root and leafy vegetables, and edible flowers. Wilbur's collection had been used to construct a wall, which created a small garden plot in front of the house. It was Wilbur's first wall, and the one which drew attention from neighbors and subsequent offers to construct stone walls on their properties. Rock had given Wilbur purpose.

Eli and Lori appeared to be in a very serious conversation with voices low and Lori showing an expression of concern, perhaps even worry. Their sister-like friendship had deepened when Eli became a true member of the Abraham family after her parents abandoned her when she was a senior in high school. There was no taboo subject between them. When Eli divorced Wilbur's father, she relied on Lori for counsel and support. When Lori married Hiram, she turned to Eli to ask if she should change her last name and whether or not it was a good idea to marry a Jewish professor of philosophy. "I'm a pediatrician, and I'm not sure if the two sciences will mix over time." Eli assured Lori that her marriage was destined for success because she and Hiram actually talked "about stuff like that."

"Hi, mom. It must be Wednesday because Lori is here. What's doing?"

Lori said, "It's our weekly talk-about-you day."

"Well, go on. I'm going to get cleaned up. I've got a dinner date tonight."

"A date? Someone we know?" asked Lori.

"Actually, we just met this afternoon. I'm doing that wall over by the middle school, and Sam, who teaches science, happened by while I was working. She even tried placing a stone, which she dropped and barely missed breaking her foot."

"Another rock head," kidded Wilbur's mother.

"Yep, but not as hard," said Wilbur.

Wilbur initially took Sam to Jake's Steaks, but, when they arrived, Sam told him that, while she wasn't a vegetarian, preferred a "less meat-centric restaurant." Wilbur was impressed with Sam speaking up without being demanding and with a gentle, polite manner. They ended up at an Indian restaurant where they shared a vegetarian pakora, orders of shrimp and lamb curries and an ample supply of garlic naan. It turned out that Sam could care less about garlic breath and couldn't get enough naan.

"I love bread. It's my go-to meal of choice. And since we won't be kissing tonight, I'll enjoy the garlic."

"We won't," asked Wilbur sheepishly.

"I don't usually go in that direction on a first date. In fact, we'll split the bill."

"You don't usually, eh? And I'm all for going Dutch."

"Right, not usually."

They reached that point in the conversation when they realized just how easy their conversation had become. Light banter flowed through more serious talk. Wilbur listened with an openness that Sam rarely experienced. She told Wilbur about her family and the warmth between her parents and her older brother. She came from a family of teachers. Her parents, who lived several hours north, were approaching retirement. Her brother taught high school in Chicago and was extremely active in social justice causes.

Wilbur filled in Sam on his own family background, his special relationship with Sal, who was really more of a father than his own father with whom he had a very infrequent and distant relationship. He talked about how his total separation from his father happened when he was thirteen, but, that since graduation from college, he had reestablished a polite speaking relationship with him.

"We just check in with one another from time to time to see how things are. He's busy with his work and his recent divorce from his second wife. And he no longer lives here in Bear City. He's managed to distance himself from everyone."

"That's really sad."

"I know. But my mother is wonderful. Sal and Sally are special. And my mother's best friend Lori is like an aunt and her parents like my grandparents."

"What about your mother's or father's parents?"

"Well, my mother's parents abandoned her when she was in high school. Who knows where they are? And my father's parents were never in the picture and I have no idea about their whereabouts."

After dinner, Wilbur and Sam walked about town. The streets illuminated by faux gas lamps keeping in fashion with the town's ongoing effort to maintain a quaintness appreciated by townsfolk and tourists. Most of the retail businesses were small boutiques. There was a Bear City ordinance against chain or franchised stores on Main Street. The town was determined to be unique and somewhat quirky. There were a few taverns... the term "bar" was not permitted...and restaurants open, with many of the restaurants offering sidewalk seating when the weather permitted. Wilbur and Sam continued talking about their families and work. They discovered they both enjoyed both modern and traditional string quartets, early jazz, the Beatles over the Rolling Stones, very little current popular music, and the watercolor art of Sal's wife Sally. After walking up and down Main Street three times, Sam took hold of Wilbur's hand, stopped, faced him and looked into his eyes. "I like you, Wilbur."

Wilbur arrived home to find Eli and Lori still in quiet conversation on the back porch. A variety of Chinese take-out boxes were scattered on the kitchen counter and dinner plates and individual tea pots remained on the porch table. Lori had obviously stayed for a dinner. As Wilbur approached, Lori asked about his date. Wilbur reported that it was a wonderful first date and that a second was already scheduled for the weekend.

Eli said, "That's nice."

"You two are having a long talk today. What's up?"

"Hiram is at a philosopher's conference for a few days, so it's a good time for your mom and me to chat the night away. Can you imagine what that conference must be like with realists and existentialists arguing with one another."

Wilbur laughed and added, "Maybe a bit like the arguments architects have with builders. Imagination versus practicality. Form versus function. Design versus poetry."

"Wilbur, maybe you should think of a career in stone philosophy," interjected his mother. "Would you mind clearing this table? Lori and I are almost done and then I'm off to bed."

"And I have a full day tomorrow," said Lori.

"And I have a wall to build," added Wilbur. At that moment, Wilbur felt that there was some sort of wall between him and his mother. He had never felt that before, but something just didn't seem right. Lori often came over on Wednesday afternoons, but he couldn't recall one time when she stayed well past dinner. She had a busy medical practice and was up early for work. The conversations between his mother and Lori were too quiet and felt secretive.

The next morning before going off to work, Wilbur sat at the kitchen island having coffee and a bowl of raisin bran when his mother entered. She looked drawn and unrested. He asked if she slept well. She said she hadn't for the last few weeks. Eli shared that she and Lori were talking about some female symptoms she was experiencing and that she would make an appointment with her doctor. She told Wilbur it was probably nothing more than what women her age typically went through. Wilbur gave his mother a hug, said he loved her, and left for work. As he hugged her, she hugged back a little firmer and longer than usual.

Wilbur and Sam went from like to love over the next five months. They learned each other's touches, smells, and tenderness. They began to make marriage plans. When Sam heard of Sal's and Sally's wedding in Eli's backyard, she insisted on a similar ceremony. They agreed that they would need to find a new place to live after the wedding. Sam's small apartment would not do. Eli offered her home, saying there was plenty of room and privacy. However, Wilbur was firm about them needing a place of their own. Lori and her family suggested they use the rustic cabin on the property that Wilbur already used as his free source of rock. He had no way of knowing that eventually he would own the real estate and replace the cabin with a slightly larger one built of stone where he and Sam would raise a daughter named for his mother.

Pop's Donuts and Coffee

The Cauldron was an eyesore at the far end of Bear City's Main Street. What had once been a restaurant specializing in stews and other hearty meals was now the town's most dilapidated structure. The exterior looked like someone, or something, had chewed most of the jade green paint off the wooden siding leaving a mottled appearance that went far beyond an excusable patina. The interior had been gutted by a dreamy-eyed investor who thought he could make it a success before he and his partners discovered significant foundation issues, along with extensive termite damage, and abandoned the building having never paid property taxes and other city fees. That's when Wendy and Dooley "Pops" Jones came along with a huge inheritance and purchased the property for one dollar at auction. They were the only bidders, and the town council was more than happy to waive back taxes and fees with the promise of a renovated building and the hope of a successful business.

It took almost a year before Wendy and Dooley were able to open Pop's Donuts and Coffee. The exterior was painted a glistening white with large windows bordered by black shutters across the front and the side of the café overlooking the river. The interior featured a long counter with fixed stools and booths with red vinyl upholstery along the windowed walls. Wendy worked the front of the house while Dooley was in charge of the kitchen. Depending on the season and the time of the day, there were two or three other employees. Besides donuts and coffee, an array of breakfast and lunch items were also on the one-page menu, but the first sensation everyone had when entering Pop's was the sweet smells of cinnamon sugar and fresh or sometimes slightly burned coffee if it was later in the morning. It was a time before gourmet coffee and fancy pastries. There wasn't a croissant in sight, nor would there be for many years to come. When Pop's opened it was an immediate success. The counter filled soon after the door was unlocked by blue- and white-collar workers on their way to their jobs. All morning, office workers came by to purchase a dozen or more "mixed" to take back to an office meeting. At lunch, the café filled with patrons ordering burgers and hot turkey sandwiches with coke, orange soda, or freshly made coffee. Late afternoon until closing at 4:00 p.m. was when the high school crowd arrived asking for sodas, French fries, and sometimes leftover donuts if any were still available. Wendy and Dooley worked long hours, rarely taking breaks, and only closing for one week each year for a well-deserved vacation, which they typically took by staying at home.

Wendy and Dooley moved to Bear City from the Midwest. They were a quiet couple, childless, and not forthcoming about their backgrounds. They were exceptionally polite and always referred to patrons by Mr. Mrs. or Miss. They quickly learned their customers names and took pride in knowing what their preferences were. "The usual" was heard more often than not. Mr. Webster, their banker and financial advisor, was the only one in town who knew the source of their inherited wealth. However, he could not figure out why they were so determined to work so hard. He was constantly urging them to hire additional help and take it easier, take a day off, take longer vacations, take time to enjoy where they lived. But Wendy and Dooley simply said they enjoyed running a popular café that served the town well.

One busy afternoon just before the end of the school year, Jack, a high school junior, asked Wendy if she might be looking for some summer help. Jack explained that he could really use a job and would be willing to do anything they might need. Wendy asked if he'd be willing to help Mr. Jones with making donuts each morning.

"You'll need to be here at 4:00 a.m. every morning, seven days a week, clean and tidy."

"I'm your guy!"

The first summer Jack worked at Pop's was grueling. Dooley was a demanding perfectionist, but, at the same time, an excellent teacher. When the summer ended and Jack was about to start his senior year, he had learned how to make the perfect donut, with a jelly-filled being the hardest and his best. He also became an expert chili cook. Dooley took pride in his family's chili recipe and insisted that Jack follow it precisely. It didn't take Jack long to figure out that there was no precision to making chili; it was all a matter of personal taste. Jack began to experiment a bit with the amounts and types of seasonings without Dooley's knowledge. One day Dooley commented that Jack's chili had finally "arrived." When Jack told Dooley what he had done, Dooley told him with a grim expression to keep doing it until told not to.

Jack came from a large Catholic family. He was one of five brothers and there were three sisters. He was the oldest and expected to lead the way through success in high school and college. His father owned a lucrative insurance agency and his mother worked part-time at Paula's Quilts and Sewing Emporium. She frequently won a blue ribbon at the county fair for her exquisite, hand-stitched quilts, often with religious or patriotic themes.

On his last day of summer employment, Wendy handed Jack his

paycheck and told him that she and Dooley expected him to return the following summer, feel free to work during any other school breaks, and was welcome to work weekends if he wanted to earn some extra money. His parents advised him to save as much as possible. By the time he finished college, he had a tidy sum in his savings account. With a degree in economics, Jack returned home without a job and returned to Pop's full-time while applying for other jobs related to his degree. Unlike many other students who had secured summer internships and moved smoothly into jobs waiting for them after graduation or onto graduate school, Jack didn't feel obligated or connected to his degree. He had fulfilled his parents' goal, but still struggled with what he wanted to do with his immediate future and certainly had no idea what to do with the rest of his life. He thought he might use some of his savings to travel, see what Europe or Africa had to offer. He didn't tend toward restlessness, but he felt there was more to just graduating college and going to work. For the most part, he had shed his religion. His parents figured that was probably part of the college experience. On Sundays when his family headed to church, he was already at Pop's making donuts and fiddling with the chili.

After about six months, Jack decided to move out of his home. He found a small, affordable apartment just a few blocks from Pop's. Working at Pop's allowed him independence and he lived frugally, not needing a car, and still able to save for whatever might come next. One chilly winter day, while Wendy was out running errands and Jack was working the front of the café during the morning lull, Phyllis walked in, removed and shook off her winter coat and hung it at the coat rack next to the entrance. She sat at a window booth with the Bear City Times opened to the help wanted section. Jack came over with a pot of coffee and a heavy beige ceramic mug, which Phyllis welcomed with a smile. She ordered a plain old-fashioned donut and began looking through the job listings.

Phyllis looked to be in her early twenties, about Jack's age, Her hair was jet black, cut short, and her eyes as black as lustrous onyx. She wore a fluffy pink sweater, which complimented her faultless complexion. When she smiled at Jack, he thought it was a smile meant only for him. He was smitten.

As he refilled her coffee mug leaving room for the generous amount of creamer and three lumps of sugar she used, he asked, "Are you looking for a job?"

"Yes. I just moved here and I'm pretty much open to just about anything."

"What brings you to Bear City?"

"My mother moved here a few months ago and I told her I'd follow after I finished with school. I'm afraid a degree in economics is not really my cup of tea."

Jack laughed at that remark and shivered at what felt like a lost opportunity to get to know the most alluring woman he had ever seen. She looked up at him with a why-did-you-laugh-at-me look. Jack quickly recaptured the moment when he said, "I'm sorry...so sorry! I wasn't laughing at you. I was really laughing at myself. I also have a degree in economics and don't know why. I'm beginning to think my future is here at Pop's."

"Are you the owner?"

"No. But I've been working here since high school and sometimes it feels like I could be." Jack returned to his spot behind the counter. Dooley came out from the kitchen to refill his coffee and had a brief quiet conversation with Jack.

Jack returned to Phyllis's table and asked, "How would you like a job here?"

Wendy and Dooley had reached that place in their lives where they wanted to slow down and even think about retirement. They had restored a wreck of a building and created a popular town meeting place. They had worked non-stop for almost thirty years. They weren't tired. In fact, their energy level remained high. However, tastes were changing. Customers were asking for gourmet coffees, a variety of pastries and healthier menu choices; all in spite of the constant demand for chili...the chili that had become Jack's "recipe."

The day that Jack and Phyllis announced their engagement was the day that Wendy and Dooley offered to sell the café. Wendy and Dooley made Phyllis and Jack an offer they couldn't refuse. Wilbur and Sal happened to be sitting at a booth when the current owners and soon-to-be new owners suddenly hugged one another. Sal was the first to offer congratulations and a suggestion that an espresso machine would make for an immediate improvement. Twelve-year old Wilbur said that no changes should be made to the old-fashioned donuts.

Pop's transition to Phyllis and Jack went smoothly. Business was always bustling, and profits increased with the addition of fancy coffees and more upscale pastries. Croissants, baked in the classic tradition with lots of buttery layers by a diminutive French woman in her home kitchen, were even on the menu. They even outsold old-fashioned and jelly donuts.

Newlyweds Phyllis and Jack hired additional staff including an experienced manager who could take over when Phyllis and Jack took regular days off. Jack's only caveat was "don't mess with the chili."

Wendy and Dooley dropped by one mid-morning during the usual lull between the breakfast and lunch crowds. They were still full of energy and seemed a bit younger than the last time they had come by. They surprised Phyllis by ordering croissants and espressos. They informed Phyllis and Jack that they were going to be going away soon but were not forthcoming about their plans.

"We're actually a bit up in the air about specifics. We're trying to be spontaneous," said Wendy, as Dooley nodded while pulling apart his croissant and slathering it with strawberry jam.

"This is really good," said Dooley. "Maybe we should have put these on the menu, but I don't think folks even knew what they were when we owned the place."

The Bear City police could never figure out how a brand-new minivan ended up in the river with Wendy and Dooley still strapped into their seatbelts and the storage area fully packed with suitcases and other travel gear. The three bridges that crossed the river were intact and no tire tracks were found leading into the river. Toxicology reports didn't indicate any kind of drug or alcohol use. It was a mystery that would forever be unsolved.

Sal Undoes at 75

There were two large storage cabinets in the garage filled with photographic equipment and paraphernalia: every camera Sal had ever used from his homemade pinpoint constructed from a shoebox painted black inside and out with a foil aperture, several vintage Kodak Brownie cameras, a pre-WW II Leica purchased for $4.00 at a garage sale, several Polaroids, and a Rolleiflex given to him by his grandfather for his sixteenth birthday. There was also a collection of darkroom equipment along with printers he used when he switched to digital photography. His most treasured item was his collection of color and black and white Kodak, Fuji and Polaroid film, several cases of each, which he stored in a refrigerator used only for his perishable photographic supplies. He began hording film when digital became the norm. He felt that there might be a time when he would return to the pleasure of working with what he called "the art of photography."

Sitting at Pop's one morning enjoying a latte and a croissant with apricot jam, he and Wilbur were talking about Wilbur's latest project. The city council had just hired Wilbur to build a wall in a newly established park. They asked Wilbur to include an archway similar to the one he had constructed on the Watson's property and also design the wall with varied elevations to allow for climbing by the kids.

Wilbur took a sip of his black coffee and said, "This will be a fun summer project and Elizabeth is excited to help."

"She's growing up so fast," said Sal. "She starts high school next term. Right?"

Wilbur thought about his mother Eli and what it must have been like to start high school without a sense of home. His mother would be so proud of the home and security he and Sam had given her granddaughter. After Eli's death, her best friend Lori had very much become a grandmother to Elizabeth and a second mother-in-law for Sam.

Wilbur replied with a beaming smile, "She's an absolute hard-headed joy."

They continued chatting about Elizabeth and how proud they both were of her empathy and care toward others. She had recently joined a student group focused on supporting the small, but needy, homeless community in Bear City. Both Wilbur and Sam had developed a reputation as civic activists and Elizabeth appeared to be following their model.

"She has also developed something of an obsession. It's not unlike ours, flowers and rocks, but, for Elizabeth, it's sandwiches. Sam and I never know what concoction she'll think of next. Yesterday she made a peanut butter and egg salad on a banana-nut muffin," said Wilbur.

Sal said, "Well, that is a bit unusual. I remember my grandfather, who gave me the Rollieflex, had a penchant for unusual sandwiches. One of his favorites was canned sardines…only the ones packed in olive oil… and thinly sliced white onions on Wonder Bread. Actually, they weren't all that bad."

Wilbur and Sal continued to enjoy their coffee and Sal even ordered another croissant. With all the donuts, pastries, and now croissants that Sal consumed, it was a wonder that he stayed slim and, according to his doctor, healthy for a man much younger than seventy-five.

The conversation shifted to Sal's photography. Sal elevated a simple photograph to a level of uncommon art. He had a way of positioning and lighting flower blossoms that made many of them seem ethereal and mystical. One of his signed prints of a dahlia had sold for an unheard-of sum that stunned the local art community. His wife Sally, a noted watercolor painter, had never sold a piece of her art for so much. Sal told Wilbur that he was going to select the same flowers already in his collection and photograph them using newly imagined arrangements.

"What are you thinking?" asked Wilbur.

"I'm going to undo the flowers by carefully taking them apart and rearranging their individual parts before taking the picture. And I'm going to use my older cameras. I may even try a pinhole camera if I can overcome several challenges. Mostly, I think I'll use the Rollieflex for color and old Brownies for black and white."

"Is this what happens when you turn 75? You start undoing things?"

"I think it's the nature of art," said Sal. "You spend a lifetime trying to bring meaning through constructed order, even abstract art attempts to find connections. Sometimes the connections are with disconnections. It's the ambivalence of art. Then it's time to find meaning through disorder and rearrangement. At least, that's my way of seeing the world and my own purpose. Don't your walls do the same?"

"Well, the putting together part, yes. I'm not so sure the taking apart accomplishes anything."

Sal said, "I think nature ultimately takes care of that through disintegration and new growth."

The first blossom Sal deconstructed was a Shasta daisy. Using a magnifier and surgical tweezers he carefully removed the petals from the central disc. He arranged the flower parts on a sheet of a non-reflective black mat so that they resembled an exploding star. He paid special attention to each petal's position so that the total effect had a sense of movement. Using the Rollieflex camera his grandfather had given him, he loaded it with Kodak color film that had a 1968 expiration date. Time and temperature would determine its quality once he processed it in his darkroom. Only natural light streaming in from the adjacent window lit the scene. Sal took eight exposures using the entire roll of film, each from a slightly different distance and angle. After taking the color pictures, he used an old Brownie to take eight black and white photos, also using the entire roll. Once he was in the darkroom, he processed both rolls and printed contact proofs before deciding which color picture he would print for show and sale. He would end up producing twenty-five signed and numbered pictures.

The black and white proofs he examined with his wife Sally. Together they would select a black and white proof that Sal would print on paper that would take watercolor paint. Sally would hand color that print, also creating twenty-five signed and numbered hand-colored prints. Each version was unique and often with colors not found in nature for that particular flower. So far, they had created over thirty pair of color and hand-colored pictures which were popular attractions and sold well at the art shows and fairs they worked. Additionally, Sally was a much in-demand watercolor artist and maintained a backlog of commissioned requests. After Eli's death, Lori continued to commission paintings from Sally, which she added to the ones Eli had bequeathed to her.

Shortly after Wilbur and Sam announced their engagement, Wilbur's mother Eli disclosed that she had been diagnosed with stage four ovarian cancer that had already spread to other organs. One sunny Sunday morning, she asked Wilbur to bring Sam over for lunch.

"I promise not to do take-out. I won't subject you or Sam to my cooking," joked Eli knowing that she had a reputation for serving prepackaged and often toaster or microwavable food. "There's something very important we need to discuss."

Shortly after Wilbur and Sam arrived and were seated at the patio table, Eli's closest friend Lori arrived carrying a large box of sandwiches and salads from a new Jewish-style deli that had just opened in town. A few minutes later Sal and Sally showed up. Wilbur looked questioningly at Sam who shrugged her shoulders in response.

"Mom, what's the surprise? Sam and I just got engaged and I hope this isn't a surprise engagement party."

"No, unfortunately it's not," said Eli.

That's when Sal interjected and went on to relate that Eli had asked him to explain the difficult situation she was in. Sal had a way of gentle communication with a clear, understandable voice. With Sally's hand on his shoulder and Lori's arm around Eli's, he filled in Wilbur and Sam of Eli's illness. Sam leaned into Wilbur quietly weeping as the story unfolded. Wilbur's eyes filled with tears as he inhaled sobs. Eli appeared calm and stoic throughout and, when Sal had finished, she reached across the table to hold Wilbur's hand. She gave a tight-lipped smile and told Wilbur she was at peace. Keeping a kind gaze into Wilbur's eyes she went on to explain some arrangements she had already made knowing that her death would probably come quickly. She did not want to endure treatments that might only extend her life with pain and indignity.

"I've made decisions about what's best for me and I hope what's best for you and Sam. I'm afraid I probably won't be alive for your wedding or certainly alive to enjoy any future grandchildren. But, Wilbur, you have brought me more joy than anyone could ever hope for. And, Sam, you have added to that joy and I know you and Wilbur will have a wonderful life together."

For the next couple of hours, with the box of sandwiches and salads left untouched, Eli laid out what she had already done. She knew that Wilbur and Sam wanted to establish their own home and hoped to build one where the cabin now existed on the "rock property."

"Lori and Hiram are buying the house, fully furnished and with any pieces of Sally's art that you may not want. It's a way of keeping the property in the family. Afterall, Lori is really my sister and your aunt. And this way, your wedding plans don't have to change. You will be married here in the garden. And Lori's family has agreed to sell the river acreage to you. The sale of this house will more than cover the cost and leave a healthy sum for building the stone house you've been planning. And don't forget you will also inherit a sizeable fortune thanks to the settlement I arranged with your father. I'll be informing him of all these changes, although I really don't have to. It's the right thing to do."

Eli told Wilbur and Sam all of this in a matter-of-fact manner. She said she had already made all the legal arrangements with her attorney. And no one needed to worry about anything having to do with her estate.

"All I want, Wilbur, is for you and Sam to be happy and spend as much time as you can with me before I go into what the doctors are saying will be a rapid decline since I've decided to not undergo any treatment."

There are times when silence best communicates indescribable feelings. Other than some quiet tears, the conversation paused. Wilbur put his arm around Sam and pulled her close. Sal and Sally were now holding hands. At almost 60, Sal was not much older than Eli. He had always thought he was closer to understanding the limits of mortality, but now realized Eli was the one with that intimate knowledge.

He broke the silence, "We love you Eli. We are here for you."

"But isn't there anything they can do?" asked Wilbur with a sense of disbelief.

"It's all too speculative and I don't want the quality of my life to be like that. I'm already taking some pain medication and I know it will be continuously increased. Lori and I have had long conversations about this. She'll be here, along with Sal and Sally, to help me. This has been going on for months. If it had been caught early on, then treatments might have had a chance."

Eli died in her own bed surrounded by her family, the family that formed after her own parents abandoned her and Lori's family took her in as one of their own. Lori's parents insisted on sitting shivah in honor of Eli. It wasn't a traditional shivah, for the Abrahams were not traditional Jews. There were no low chairs, mirrors were not covered, folks were free to come and go, and no rabbi was even summoned. Doctor and Mrs. Abraham explained it was a time to mourn, remember and celebrate Eli's life as a family.

"Think of it as an elongated Jewish wake," said Dr. Abraham. "Our culture has always been good at figuring things out in the moment and even beginning new traditions well in advance of them becoming traditions. Besides, in our eyes, Eli was a member of our tribe."

Fifteen years passed. Wilbur, Sam and their teenager Elizabeth live by the river in the stone cabin Wilbur built while Lori, Hiram and their two children keep Eli's home almost the same as when they moved in. The backyard is lush with color and Wilbur's first wall in the front yard remains as a lasting memorial to Eli, where some of her ashes were spread after her death. Wilbur had decided that Sally's watercolors should stay with the home. It was all part of their extended family with "Aunt" Lori. Sal was immersed in his undoing. His photos of disassembled flowers had grown and increased in popularity along with Sally's reimagined colorization of the black and white prints.

On the anniversary of Eli's passing, Wilbur, Sam, Elizabeth,

Sal, Sally and Lori sat in the large corner booth at Pop's; gathering in remembrance of Eli had become an annual ritual. Lori even brought a yahrzeit candle.

"It's not religious. It's just a candle," said Lori. "My family seems to always have a supply."

Phyllis came over and remarked, "I see it's that time of the year again. Where's Hiram today?"

Lori said he was at another philosopher's conference. "He's getting some sort of honor for his latest paper 'Jews, Words and Punctuation.'"

Phyllis, with her quick wit, said, "How do philosophers honor one another? Do they first have a long debate about the nature of honor? Do they delve into why or why not awards should be given? Is recognition in their vocabulary?"

"I think you are getting into some important unresolved areas," said Sal with a wink. "For me, at this moment in the history of this particular point in the timeline of the universe…not trying to be too philosophical… I'm more interested in an espresso and one of the delicious croissants that Madame Francine bakes fresh for you each morning."

The entire table laughed much too loud and Phyllis, with a flourish threw her arms up in the air, and said, "Touché!"

Even though it was lunchtime, Sal's order never seemed to change much. Sally asked for a fried egg sandwich, Lori a recent menu addition salad niçoise, Wilbur and Sam wanted to split an Impossible burger with a green salad, and then it was Elizabeth's turn.

She asked Phyllis what kind of chili Jack had made for the day. Phyllis said it was meat without beans and moderately spicy. That's when Elizabeth surprised the table by asking if Jack could cut a croissant in two and slather chili over the halves.

"And I'd like an orange soda, too."

"Well, that sounds interesting and I'm sure Jack will do that," said Phyllis.

Sally looked at Elizabeth and told her she was being awfully creative and wondered if she had any idea what that concoction might taste like. Sam added that it was interesting to experiment with food as long as it wasn't wasted. Lori beamed and said that Eli would be very proud of her granddaughter's uniqueness.

When their food arrived, Jack came out from the kitchen to personally present Elizabeth's sandwich invention. Using a knife and fork, she took a bite and proclaimed it, "very, very tasty."

"Well, then," said Jack. "We'll name it the "Eli" and put it up on the special's board from time to time."

Sal reminisced, "When your dad was younger than you, he called me a flower bandit and thought of himself as a rock bandit. It was all about appreciating uniqueness in ourselves and in others. That's what growing up is all about. I think that maybe you might be a sandwich bandit."

Elizabeth thought about what Sal said and replied, "Perhaps.

Elizabeth Takes Charge

Wilbur and Sal sat in their favorite booth at Pop's Donuts and Coffee. Sal enjoying an early morning espresso and cheese danish while Wilbur had plain black coffee. Dark clouds hung low in an October sky. There had already been early snow in the surrounding mountains and the river dividing Bear City was running higher than average. It looked to be a wet year that had the potential to break a two-year drought. Fortunately, there were few summer fires and a fairly smoke-free season. Wilbur had just finished building a second wall on the Watson property, which ran perpendicular to the one he had built almost a dozen years before that divided the Watsons' two homes. Sal and Sally were in the midst of preparing photos and watercolors for the annual Fall Art Festival held in the town's central plaza. The aroma of cinnamon and vanilla was particularly strong and Pop's owners Phyllis and Jack seemed to be in a funk. Phyllis was not being her normal exuberant self and had yet to refill Wilbur's coffee mug.

"Elizabeth should be here soon," said Wilbur. "She's earned a short vacation. She's been working extremely long hours for a first-year attorney, but her firm is very appreciative of the work she's been doing."

Sal asked, "Is it the same firm she interned while in law school?"

"Yes, and it's really her dream job. She's already assisted in several civil rights cases, which is the work she has always wanted to do. Her friends keep telling her there's no money in civil rights, but she's determined to make a difference."

"Well, that's the daughter you raised," commented Sal. "She's always been a force of nature."

Elizabeth graduated from high school when she was sixteen, earned a bachelor's degree in political science with honors, finished law school at the top of her class and passed the state bar exam all by the time she was twenty-three. Each summer she interned at a medium-sized law firm where she had a chance to learn the mechanics of being an attorney, and also work with several noted civil rights attorneys. It wasn't working with the ACLU, which she thought would be her dream job, but it was very close. Almost all her work was pro bono with clients from mostly minority populations who did not have the means to afford a private attorney. She deeply appreciated working at a value- and purpose-driven law firm that put significant resources toward civil rights law and was thrilled when they invited her to formally join the firm after graduation.

Elizabeth arrived along with her mother Sam. There were times when they dressed alike and could be mistaken as twin sisters. Wilbur wondered what happened to his genes. Mother and daughter were both tall, slender and self-assured. Elizabeth had outgrown her early shyness and now behaved with the same self-assuredness as Sam. Although Elizabeth had never known her Grandmother Eli, she clearly inherited her empathy and compassion for the underdog. Elizabeth and Sam had alluring green eyes capable of capturing a room's attention.

Wilbur stood and hugged Elizabeth telling her how good it was to have her home for a short visit. Sam and Elizabeth slid into one side of the booth and Wilbur sat next to Sal and across from his wife and daughter. Phyllis approached and asked for Sam and Elizabeth's order. Sam said she'd have a latte. Elizabeth asked what kind of chili Jack had made for the day and Phyllis said ground beef with a mix of kidney and cannellini beans. She added that it was extra spicy. Elizabeth asked for a chili and cheese omelet, a small glass of tomato juice, and a double espresso. Phyllis leaned over and quietly asked if she could have a private chat with Elizabeth after she delivered the order to Jack. Elizabeth maintained a neutral expression before excusing herself and moving to a booth across the café. Her parents and Sal looked at each other questioningly before Sal said, "I wonder what that's all about?"

"Phyllis called me this morning after you left, Wilbur. She said something about an employee problem and knew Elizabeth would be in town today. She asked me if it would be okay if she could talk with Elizabeth. I told her we were joining the two of you soon," said Sam.

Elizabeth returned to the table and Phyllis brought over their orders. Elizabeth promised Phyllis that she wouldn't tell Sal and her parents that she and Jack might be sued by an individual claiming he was discriminated against when not offered employment.

Richard lived just outside town on a small boutique farm. His parents Reggie and Cora Ellison owned a small market where they featured their home-grown fruits and vegetables. Their store had become a go-to source of heirloom produce as well as a variety of imported foods. His parents had high expectations for him and his two younger sisters. Reggie and Cora expected that all three would go to college, a privilege neither of them had growing up. Their store did well, but they also expected their children to earn a portion of their college expenses.

Richard began working at Pop's Donuts and Coffee as a junior in high school, just as Jack had done. Phyllis and Jack both found him to be an exemplary employee. He was asked back each summer and also given as many weekend and school break hours as he could manage. Even with several college scholarships, Richard came to depend on working at Pop's to cover the gap between those scholarships and the real cost of attending a first-rate university. Richard and his family were one of the few Black families in Bear City. For the most part, townsfolk thought of them as examples of overcoming prejudice through hard work and perseverance.

When the Bear City Chamber of Commerce recognized Reggie and Cora with their annual Business of the Year Award, the mayor said, "You serve as an example of what minorities can achieve when they just put their minds to it." Reggie and Cora both smiled, accepted their award, and with simple dignity thanked the Chamber. When they got home, Richard asked how the dinner had gone and his parents explained that it was another example of good intentions gone awry. Conversations about race, difference, intolerance, and personal safety were a normal part the Ellison's family life. They enjoyed living in a small self-described progressive town, even though those who described themselves as progressives often used the label to obscure entitlement and separateness.

Elizabeth's family frequented Reggie and Cora's market. Elizabeth was five years older than Richard but remembered him sweeping the market's floors and stocking shelves. When she drove up the hardpacked dirt lane to his home and parked on a graveled area, he was sitting on the front porch of a sunny yellow and white trimmed two-story house. A low stone wall interrupted by three wooden steps crossed in front of the porch. It housed a collection of kitchen herbs covered by a loose netting to discourage various animals from feasting on tasty greens. A large strawberry patch was off to the right of the house; to the left was a small, neatly maintained grove of fruit trees. She immediately recognized Richard. He stood, all six foot two, sporting a short Afro and a toned build kept in shape from playing club lacrosse. One of his sports heroes was Jim Brown, who was a legendary lacrosse player at Syracuse University before becoming a Hall of Fame running back with the Cleveland Browns.

"You must be Richard. I'm Elizabeth."

"Hello. Come on up. I've been waiting since your phone call."

"I recognized you from when you worked at your parents' store. I suppose you are home for the weekend. I hear you are at the university and doing well."

"I hear you are a successful attorney. Are you representing Pop's? Because, if you are, we shouldn't talk unless my attorney is present."

"Do you have an attorney?" inquired Elizabeth.

"Not yet officially. I'm talking to a few, but there doesn't seem to be one in town willing to represent me. So maybe I need to keep quiet until I do."

"Why do you think you can't find representation in town?"

"Why do you think?" responded Richard.

Elizabeth told Richard that she was not formally representing Phyllis and Jack. She explained that they had asked but she told them she only represented plaintiffs.

"However, I'll be happy to talk to Richard and see if what you call a misunderstanding can be worked out before it becomes a full-fledged legal issue."

Phyllis and Jack were deeply troubled by Richard's accusation that they had discriminated against him when they hired someone else for the summer. It all went back to when Wendy and Dooley sold Pop's to Phyllis and Jack. Wendy and Dooley had no immediate family known by anyone in town. Dooley revealed that he did have an estranged brother living on the other side of the country and had been trying to reconcile with him for several years. As part of the healing process, he promised his brother that there would always be a job at Pop's for any relative. When he sold Pop's, he required Phyllis and Jack to honor that commitment as long as they owned the cafe. For all the years they've had Pop's, they knew that their moral commitment to Dooley was firm. When Dooley's nephew showed up one early spring day and explained how he knew of Dooley's promise, Phyllis and Jack believed they had no choice but to hire him.

"Informing Richard that he would not have his summer job was heart wrenching," said Phyllis. "But we made a commitment to Dooley."

"Couldn't you hire two extra summer employees?" asked Elizabeth.

Jack said, "As well as we do, business is still tight. And, for now, Dooley's distant relative will be more than just a summer employee. He's in a bit of a bind with his own family and is looking to stay in Bear City until things get worked out. We just don't have the resources for two extra employees. The deli down the street has really impacted our business and we're struggling a bit."

Elizabeth thought about the situation when Phyllis said, "We even found another job for Richard. The deli was willing to take him on, but Richard said the oddest thing 'separate but equal is not equal.'"

"Actually, that isn't so odd," said Elizabeth.

Elizabeth shared Phyllis and Jack's dilemma with Richard. However, Richard was firm in his belief that a promise made so many years ago was not an excuse for favoritism. He expressed his affection for Phyllis and Jack and felt they had always been kind to him. Richard spoke with a calm resolve. Elizabeth saw him as an intelligent and thoughtful man. She found it difficult to accept that race was a factor.

"You believe that you've been discriminated against because you're Black," stated Elizabeth.

"I don't believe that Phyllis and Jack see themselves as racists. In fact, I didn't see them that way until they had a choice to make. Whether they know it or not, they are using the promise as an excuse. Sure, it presents a moral and ethical conflict for them, but they're using history to justify the current situation. Black people experience that story every day. Change won't happen until white folks understand and change that behavior."

Elizabeth listened. She intentionally kept her facial expression neutral, cocked her head slightly to one side and nodded affirmatively as Richard spoke. She purposefully used her body language to invite Richard's narrative. As Richard talked, she reflected on her own work as an advocate for those confronting civil rights abuses. Yet, she sensed her own inner conflict between Richard's experience and how she knew Phyllis and Jack. Elizabeth felt a chilly shudder of insecurity and ambiguity. She wanted to take charge of an emotionally explosive situation but wasn't sure how to proceed.

"I'd really like to help all of you work through this, but I'm not sure I'm the right person. Would it be alright with you if I think about this for a bit and get back to you? I give you my word, I'm not going to go back into town and talk to Phyllis and Jack until we meet again. I just need some time. I do feel certain allegiances here, but I want to be fair."

"I've heard that before," said Richard. "But I'll give you the benefit of the doubt."

"Actually, I'd like to talk this over with my folks, if that's alright with you."

"I know Wilbur and Sam. Your folks are good people. Did you know that your dad helped my father build that little stone wall?" asked Richard while pointing at the structure across from the patio. "They did it all in one afternoon and your dad brought all the stone in exchange for some fruit and veggies."

"I didn't," replied Elizabeth. "I wonder what he might have done if he had a choice between helping your father and helping a white person."

"I suppose we'll have to wonder," said Richard.

On her way home, Elizabeth thought about something one of her

Black colleagues said to her when they were discussing race. Elizabeth thought of herself as a rational person who could look at issues from multiple perspectives before coming to a conclusion. As a woman, she often grappled with men who held on to the myth that women's emotions interfered with logic. It surprised her when her colleague asserted that the difference between how a Black person thought about race was far different from a white person.

"We think more with our hearts, and you with your brain," said George, one of the partners in Elizabeth's law firm. "Our history is filled with heartfelt, often gut-wrenching experiences that can't be explained with any sense of logic. It has been the work of pure evil. You want to understand and think through events. You can afford to be distant and unemotional. Yes, I know you are empathetic, and that's important and appreciated, but it will never be enough to feel the intensity of injustice and persistent discrimination. White folks have learned to tolerate, but they haven't learned to embrace, immerse, and ultimately grasp what it's like to live in my skin."

It was a profound experience for Elizabeth. She continued to have long conversations with George. Her empathy deepened but never crossed the line to actual experience. She came to believe that tolerance was an excuse to maintain sympathetic and respectful distance. She was beginning to feel injustice and not simply understand it. Now she was faced with having to make a choice between friendship and respect. She knew that Phyllis and Jack probably had the law on their side. They owned a small, private business and could employ anyone without needing to give a reason for their decision. They didn't owe Richard an explanation. It would be easy for Elizabeth to tell Richard he didn't have a case if she didn't also feel that Richard deserved more respect than he had been given. In her mind, Richard's history carried more weight than Dooley's relative.

By the time Elizabeth arrived home, the sky had cleared, and she saw her father down by the river gathering river rock. A late afternoon fall crispness was filled with a sweet smell of the woods bordering the far side of the river. The river was running lower than normal, and it was easy to gather the rocks. She walked down and began lifting stone onto the fully restored 1947 Ford one-ton flatbed truck. From Elizabeth's silent demeanor, Wilbur knew she was struggling with what Phyllis had shared with her. After Elizabeth and Sam left Pop's, Phyllis sat in the booth with Wilbur and Sal and explained the situation.

"I just don't know what Jack and I could have done differently," said

Phyllis. Her hands quivered and her lips were tight.

Sal said, "You and Jack want to do the right thing. Sometimes there are two kinds of right. You've got a lot to figure out."

Wilbur loaded a few more rocks in the truck before turning to Elizabeth. "Phyllis shared the problem with me and Sal after you left this morning. Are you thinking of representing Phyllis and Jack? Is there really a case against them?"

"I'm not going to represent either Richard or Phyllis and Jack. I don't think there's a legal case. That's probably why Richard hasn't found representation. I doubt any attorney in town would take the case. I just came from meeting with Richard. I'm trying to think of how to approach all three of them."

Wilbur and Elizabeth walked up to the stone cabin Wilbur had built shortly after he and Sam were married. He had recently extended the front porch and Sal had surrounded it with rhododendrons, hydrangeas and freeway roses. A large redwood picnic table was set with a blue and yellow oilcloth tablecloth and Sam announced that chicken enchiladas were in the oven and a large salad already made.

"Do we have enough for a guest?" asked Elizabeth.

"We have plenty," said Sam.

"Let me make a phone call. Can we wait an hour?"

Forty-five minutes later, Richard drove up and was welcomed by Elizabeth and her parents. They sat at the table enjoying the enchiladas and salad Wilbur had made. A large pitcher of iced tea along with a supply of corn tortillas completed the menu.

"We would have had more if Elizabeth had told us in advance that we'd have a guest," said Wilbur.

"This is really good," said Richard. "Have you seen my mom and dad lately? You do shop at the market, don't you?"

"We see Reggie and Cora all the time," said Sam. "In fact, most of what we're having for dinner came from the market."

Elizabeth mentioned that she had seen the wall that her father helped Richard's father build.

She asked, "Dad, if you had a choice between helping the Ellison's and a white family, what would you have done?"

Richard was taken aback. "I'm not sure you should ask that question while I'm sitting here."

"Why not? We talked about it earlier. How can we know anything if we keep silent?"

Wilbur interrupted, "I'm okay with the question. Richard, you ought to know that Elizabeth is not shy about bringing up anything. We actually love that about her. And I don't know what I'd do. I'd like to think that race wouldn't have been the deciding factor, but I really don't know."

Elizabeth said, "Dad, I'd like to think you'd find a way to help both families without having to choose. It's choices that force the issue. I think choices are like walls." Elizabeth went on to say that some walls serve to create spaces with a particular and exclusive function. Then she told Richard about the wall that her father built on the Watson's property.

"The Watsons live in two separate houses and wanted a wall to divide their property. They also wanted a gate so that they could have easy access to one another. I helped my dad with that wall and the archway for the gate. At first, I thought it was strange having a wall that didn't intend to keep folks apart. In fact, I think it actually served to bring two people closer together. What kind of wall describes what's going on between you and Phyllis and Jack?"

Wilbur and Sam stood and cleared the dinner plates and leftover food. Sam said that dessert would be served soon. Elizabeth and Richard continued talking in low voices. Wilbur came back and put a collection of small stones at the center of the table just as Phyllis and Jack drove up the driveway.

Richard said, "Is this a set-up, Elizabeth?"

"Yes, just a bit. But, please, play along. I promise I'm not trying to trick anyone into anything. Well, maybe a little bit," she said with a half-smile.

Phyllis and Jack walked over carrying a cherry pie. "We've brought dessert and, as request by Elizabeth, open minds."

Everyone sat at the table. Richard and Elizabeth across from Phyllis and Jack and Wilbur and Sam at opposite ends.

"My dad is really good at building walls, walls that serve all sorts of purposes. Walls that divide, walls for play, walls that invite entry, walls that stoke the imagination, walls that are functional and poetic." Elizabeth turned to her father with a broad smile and added, "Yes, dad, I know you like poetry to be part of your walls." Elizabeth picked up a stone from the center of the table and took charge, "In some parts of the world stones are used to hurt, humiliate, and even kill others who think differently or are different. My dad uses stone to create beauty and often peace and tranquility. Here's a small pile of stones. I'd like to ask the three of you," nodding to Richard, Phyllis and Jack, "to build a wall across the center of this table one stone at a time with each of you taking one turn at a time. While you build that wall, I'd like you to talk about what each stone represents, the kind of wall you are building or tearing down or opening up. What do you want your futures to be?"

And so, they did.

Lori Buys a Pastrami Sandwich

Lori stood at the counter of Moshe's Deli looking over an array of meats and salads trying to decide what to order. Lori was going to meet her husband Hiram at the university for lunch and Hiram always had a turkey and swiss on rye, mayo only, no tomatoes, a bag of Fritos and a cream soda.

"There are so many choices. I just can't decide," said Lori.

"So, Hiram is having his usual. Might I suggest a nice hot pastrami with coleslaw on rye, one of our house-made kosher dills on the side, and your usual iced tea."

"That sounds good, but I'll need to run a few extra miles to burn it all off," joked Lori. She was one of the lucky high metabolism women who never seemed to gain weight. Hiram, on the other hand, was always fighting his waistline and over the years had developed the middle-aged bulge a bit ahead of schedule. Lori and Hiram met for lunch every Wednesday afternoon when he had a long break between teaching philosophy and keeping office hours and she worked a shortened day at her medical practice. When her closest friend Eli was alive, Wednesday afternoons were their times to get together.

When it opened, Moshe's Deli became an instant success. Bear City had a significant Jewish population and, before Moshe's, an unrequited appetite for corned beef, pastrami, corn rye bread, chewy bagels, knishes, and other Jewish delicacies. There were two synagogues for those who espoused their cultures while, at the same time, being generally irreverent. Temple Beth Shalom was a more traditional reform synagogue where some of the service was in Hebrew and the sermons long and didactic. It was not unusual after services to find Rabbi Rosenthal surrounded by members of the congregation in fervent, finger-pointing argument over the inaccuracy and faulty logic of his sermons. The other synagogue was a temple without a building. It was more of a community gathering place for "seekers of truth and beauty" according to Rabbi Simon Chapman who wore his gray hair in a man bun and smoked a briar pipe much to the dismay of his itinerant congregation. Hebrew-minimum services were held in the round at free public open spaces whenever "the need arose." Intoned mantras were the norm rather than debate and conflict. According to Hiram, the long-standing tradition of Jewish argument was well entrenched in Beth Shalom and sadly absent in the alternative "no-name, no blame" roving Jewish-in-name-only community.

Lori's family eschewed all religion while keeping alive cultural traditions, especially food and family gatherings. They belonged to neither synagogue because, in their opinion, groupthink was dangerous. Lori followed her family's lead by keeping certain rituals alive without any piety. Hiram, being something of a new-age philosopher, felt an obligation to acknowledge his own Jewishness while creating personal and, like Lori, family rituals. One of those personal rituals being the current order at Moshe's Deli. Another being breakfast at Pop's Donuts and Coffee with the family on Saturday mornings.

"It's our obligation to spread our wealth between Pop's and Moshe's. No favorites," proclaimed Hiram. "We must find balance in our lives whenever possible."

Lori found Hiram's cliched aphorisms quaintly appealing. She once mentioned to Sal's wife Sally, "I know he's a bit kooky, but he's my kooky cookie."

Moshe handed Lori the order and asked, "It's Wednesday. Meeting Hiram for lunch?"

"Yes. And, since it's such a beautiful day, we'll picnic outside."

"In that case, let me throw in a couple of rugalach for dessert. Fresh this morning."

Hiram already had a blanket spread out under a huge oak tree, which they called their Picnic Tree. Lori set the deli bags down, gave Hiram a brief kiss hello, and began pulling out food and beverages.

"Here's your usual. Moshe talked me into a hot pastrami, and he threw in a couple of goodies for dessert. Have you been here long?"

"I just arrived. It's a perfect day and I have some interesting news to share."

Hiram told Lori about a surprise meeting with the town's mayor. The city council had decided it was going to create a new position: Bear City Ethics Administrator. Several council members had recently become aware of the dispute between Richard Ellison and the owners of Pop's Donuts and Coffee and felt the need to examine the town's ordinances and practices for any existing or potential discriminatory practices. Hiram was asked if he would like to be the first ethics administrator.

"The council also wants the new ethics administrator to begin a "stakeholder conversation" to address systemic racism."

Lori listened with serious interest. It had been a while since Hiram was presented with any new work. He was at that stage in his academic career where he felt he was cruising, going through the motions, and not finding unique and interesting philosophical problems to address. Her listening was interrupted by several noisy Steller's Jays, who seemed to always be around when picnickers took advantage of the Picnic Tree.

"Is this something you want to take on. It seems like a no-win situation," said Lori.

"Well, I feel something of an obligation to the community. Richard exposed one of our town's unconfronted truths. Is it a no-win issue? I'd like to think we can get beyond that kind of polarized thinking, but I really don't know. Anyway, as a Jew, I've come to expect confrontation without reason."

"Aren't you afraid of exposing other truths? Anti-Semitism? Ageism? Misogyny? And a longer list of -isms the town might choose to regret and ignore?"

Hiram thought about his life's work. He had spent an academic career in explorative thought. He studied the effect of words and language on human behavior, specifically on Jewish life and intellectualism. He had been a distant observer, not an intimate participant.

"I've never been shy about engaging in dialog, but I've never taken it to the next level. I also realize there are those who think of me as some sort of new-age goof. I'm good at getting my students to enjoy their studies with humor and sometimes real thinking. I'm becoming uncomfortable with treating my classroom as a minor comedy club or a venue for duels where words serve as lances. It's time to be a philosopher of action. It's time to confront ugly truths and help our community transform itself from what it falsely espouses into a more truthful reality."

Lori put down her pastrami sandwich and scooted into Hiram. "I love you for your noble cause. I tend to babies after they're born, and you'll help our town birth a new reality."

Hiram laughed and said, "You see the results of your work on a daily basis. I'm still wrestling with exactly what a diverse coalition might do. You know what's been said about what a committee accomplishes: 'A camel is a horse designed by a committee.' I think it was actually said by a car designer who hated working in teams, but it seems to fit all too often"

Now it was Lori's turn to chuckle. She held Hiram's hands affectionately, looked into his eyes, and firmly told him that, if there was anyone who could do the job, it was him.

"You're brilliant. Just don't allow your brilliance to get in the way."

After lunch, Lori had a few errands to run. First, she made a brief stop at her parents' home. Dr. and Mrs. Abraham were both in their early nineties and in excellent health. They were both avid walkers and felt unsatisfied if they didn't record at least five miles each day on their Fitbits. They looked forward to their only daughter's Wednesday drop-ins and they set the kitchen table with a freshly ironed beige tablecloth and matching napkins. When Lori arrived, Mrs. Abraham made a pot of tea and set out some freshly baked goodies.

"Are those rugalach from Moshe's?"

"They are. I didn't have time to make anything this morning, so your father and I stopped by the deli while out walking this morning," said Mrs. Abraham.

"Funny. Hiram and I had sandwiches from the deli and Moshe threw in a couple. He didn't mention you had been in earlier."

They sat at the kitchen table and Lori brought them up to date on the grandchildren and her own work as one of the town's most respected pediatricians. All of the Abraham children had followed their father into medicine, but the talk around the kitchen table was rarely about their work. It was always about family, friends, theater and politics. Mrs. Abraham still found occasional roles playing heavyset grandmotherly types with the local community theater. She was probably the most well-read member of the family when it came to history and political theory. She was never shy about voicing her opinion about the country's current political news. She could be having lunch or dinner out with friends and, if someone mentioned the president, she might loudly slap her hand on the table drawing attention from other diners and almost shouting, "Don't mention that putz's name in my presence! We should all be embarrassed by that orange-headed monster." Dr. Abraham preferred more solitary and serene activities. After retirement, he had become an avid fly fisherman and was often found quietly casting from the riverfront property he had once owned and sold to Wilbur. When Wilbur's daughter Elizabeth still lived at home, the two of them were frequent anglers with Elizabeth often catching more fish than Dr. Abraham.

Lori announced, "Hiram has been asked to be the town's first ethic's administrator. The city council wants Hiram to find any evidence of bias in city ordinances and also have him convene a diverse citizen group to address prejudice in Bear City."

"Well, that sounds like a no-win job," said Mrs. Abraham.

"And he'd better be prepared for an uptick in anti-Semitism. I hope he knows what he's getting into," added Dr. Abraham.

"He thinks he needs to stop philosophizing and be more directly involved in our town's life. Mom, you remember when Clinton began a national dialog on race?"

"A noble effort, but where did it go? Look where we are now. Pathetic."

"I think Hiram wants to move forward. Maybe it happens at the local level. When Elizabeth had Richard, Phyllis and Jack together over pie and a pile of stones, she started a dialog. She was able to push unspoken ills into the open."

The story of when Richard Ellison, one of a handful of Black residents in Bear City, felt discriminated against when the owners of Pop's Donuts and Coffee had employed a distant relative of the original owners in place of reemploying Richard had become public. Elizabeth had facilitated a deep discussion between the three of them and they came away with a much deeper understanding of the conflict and a renewed relationship. However, it wasn't until Moshe offered to help with funding an additional position that Richard was rehired. Moshe went to Phyllis and Jack and told them he knew his success had put a dent in Pop's profits, and he wanted to help even things out. Phyllis and Jack were stunned, but Moshe said that everyone should share in each other's good fortune. Moshe was praised by many and called a dangerous socialist by a few. It also marked the time when Phyllis, Jack and Moshe began eating at each other's restaurants at least twice a week. Richard also made sure his parents Reggie and Cora balanced their patronage evenly between Pop's and Moshe's.

"Smaller steps in smaller communities," said Lori.

"It sounds like a slogan," said Mrs. Abraham. "Maybe a good one. Be sure to tell Hiram."

Dr. Abraham added, "Maybe Hiram should work with Wilbur and get the town to work on a wall together while having a dialog."

"I don't think that gets to small," replied Lori.

On her way home, Lori stopped by Pop's and asked about the day's chili. Phyllis said that Jack had gone a bit crazy with a pork and venison concoction. Lori bought enough for dinner along with a couple of baguettes, which Jack had recently begun offering. The front counter at Pop's, which had once been filled with a wide variety of donuts, was increasingly featuring new bakery items. There were still Madame Francine's croissants and now Jack's baguettes and a variety of danishes. Sometimes he even offered some of Moshe's baked goods and, in return, Moshe sold Jack's bread. On her way out, Sal entered for his afternoon coffee break, even though he had been retired for years and seemed to be on an elongated break.

"Hi, Lori. I hear Hiram has a new gig bringing the town together."

"Word travels fast. How did you know?"

"Small towns, big ears and open mouths."

"No doubt," said Lori.

Hiram was at home sitting at the kitchen table with his cell phone glued to his ear. Lori placed the chili and baguettes on the counter and sat next to him. It was obvious that he was having an intense conversation with the mayor. Hiram never raised his voice, but his tone sometimes bordered on sarcasm and, with his eye rolling and raised brow, he appeared to be edging dangerously close to unwanted speech. Lori gestured calmness with her hands and Hiram quickly took the cue. He switched to listening and affirming with yesses and uh-huhs.

Disconnecting from the call he shook his head and said, "That was the mayor. He's insisting that I alone examine city ordinances and documents. I told him that would leave the process open to favoritism and criticism. He's also on edge about putting together a group of stakeholders. I'm not sure he really wants to deal with this. It's feeling like a smokescreen. I'm not sure I want to take the council up on their offer."

Lori remained quiet while Hiram contemplated the situation and looked into empty space. He was searching for answers.

"What would happen if the university became involved without the city's involvement. What would happen if you took the lead with or without the university's blessing? Forget about reviewing documents. Just convene a panel. How about forming a truth and reconciliation process similar to what Canada did over the harm done to indigenous people by the Indian Residential Schools system. I think South Africa used the process after apartheid."

Lori knew Hiram to be a gifted facilitator. She had seen him work with small groups asking open-ended and thought-provoking questions that prompted divergent and sometimes belligerent participants to reach resolution around dicey problems.

"It might lead to some sort of resolution," stated Lori.

"I'm not sure the goal is resolution. I think that might be too much to expect. It's about improving relations first. Resolution takes time and complete agreement on what's the problem," said Hiram. "But I do think you're helping me to get on the right track."

"What do you think the city wants?"

"Problems solved with a minimum of fuss," said Hiram. "I think I'll go take a walk. Did you pick up chili from Pop's? It smells delicious."

"I did. I also got some fresh baguettes. I'll put together a salad and we'll eat after you get back."

While Hiram was out walking, Lori called Elizabeth's cell, which was answered immediately. Although still at the beginning of her career, Elizabeth had already established a reputation as a fierce defender of civil rights. She shared the dilemma Hiram was facing and sought Elizabeth's advice. They were still talking when Hiram returned from his walk. He began getting out bowls, plates, and cutlery and set the table. With Lori still on the phone, he pulled together salad ingredients: two kinds of lettuce, carrots, celery, some pickled onions and cauliflower, and crumbled bleu cheese dressing. He assembled the salad, cut one baguette into ovals, reheated the chili in the microwave, and put out some sweet butter. Lori looked at him and gave the one-minute signal with her forefinger.

As they began to eat, Hiram asked what Elizabeth had to say. Lori was quick to summarize. "Basically, she said you should respectfully decline the offer from the mayor and the council and, in the words of Spike Lee, 'do the right thing.'"

"But what is the 'right thing?'"

"I asked her that very question."

"And what did she say?"

"She said you're the philosopher and you'll figure it out."

Hiram smiled. "At least she didn't suggest a wall-building exercise."

Lori smiled back. "Oh, I wouldn't necessarily say that."

Wilbur's Wall Stops a Fire

Bear City is surrounded by wilderness. For much of the year, it is lush, green meadowland gently rising to a forest of red oak, beech, maple, dogwood and madrone at the lower levels with pine forests up higher. During the summer, especially during all-too-frequent draught years, it becomes bone dry. The town's people describe it as a wick waiting to be lit, which could lead to an explosive firestorm. When thunderstorms threaten, along with dry lightning, the entire town is on edge and all available fire and forestry department personnel are put on watch. Over the years, several large fires have been stopped just short of entering town. Fortunately, those fires began when the winds were light or blowing away from town.

High school students, without summer jobs or other productive activities to keep them occupied, often spent time out in the meadows drinking beer, smoking weed, and generally partying. Most of their parents say, "It's simply kids being kids. We were like that when we were their age." Town council members, the chief of police, and the fire marshal were constantly discussing that something had to be done. Unfortunately, all the carping and finger pointing led nowhere. Much of the public debate often ended with a collective blame cast to the county government because the meadows were technically outside the city's jurisdiction. The posted Smokey Bear "Only You" warning signs were an empty warning.

It was late August, a couple of weeks before school was due to start, when a few dozen teens decided to have one last end-of-summer party. The evening was calm, mosquitos heavy, and a small campfire, which the partygoers had carefully contained within a wall of river rock, provided an eerie glow. The party was beginning to wind down and everyone began picking up their portable chairs, blankets, personal belongings, and even the empty bottles, cans, and other debris scattered about. They used a few flat stones to tamp out the campfire's dying embers and poured partially drunk beverages over the fire pit. A few boys announced they'd stay and be the last to leave so that they could pee on the fire's remnants to make sure it was fully extinguished.

The site had been abandoned for an hour or so when a late-night breeze picked up and blew a single ember that had not been extinguished by beer, soda or pee into some dry wild rye grass, which immediately blossomed into flame spreading across the meadow toward town and up the hill into the deciduous forest. Rebecca and Claude Watson were awakened by the sound of sirens and pounding knocks on their front doors with shouts to immediately evacuate. The Watson's houses were the first ones standing between the fire and town. Rebecca threw on a robe and stepped into slippers before running outside. She ran across the lawn and through the rose-covered arch in the wall that Wilbur had built towards Claude's house. Claude was already in the yard pointing to the SUV parked in the driveway. Fireman were pulling out hoses in preparation for trying to save both Watson homes when the flames suddenly ceased at the stone wall. The first responders began hosing down the flames along the wall and around Rebecca's house. Miraculously, the fire appeared to be reversing and burning back on itself. The only spread was into the forest and, without any significant wind, was moving very slowly.

Rebecca and Claude stood dumbfounded at what they had just seen. The fire marshal approached and asked if they were okay and, after staring at the scarred area where the fire had stopped, said they were in a bit of shock and very grateful for the fire crew. The marshal told them they were smart to have such a large defensible space surrounding their structures and that the wall definitely helped to stop the spread. He said the fire creeping into the forest would be quickly put out by hand crews and helicopter water drops.

"I've already heard that the forestry responders have set a line that should keep the fire from getting into the pines. We keep a fairly large contingent of fire fighters on alert during this time of the year and we were able to jump on this quickly."

"We're so appreciative," said Rebecca. "There's no telling what might have happened if the fire pushed past our property. We're not that far from town."

"We'll shut down this part of the operation within an hour and it's safe for you to remain here. My guess is that the remaining fire will be fully controlled within the next day or two. Since the weather is favorable right now and there is no significant change in the forecast, you should be just fine."

The next morning, Wilbur and Elizabeth, pulled into the Watson's driveway. Wilbur heard from Sal during morning coffee at Pop's Donuts and Coffee about the fire.

"Your wall kept the fire from advancing," reported Sal. "It's the one you and Elizabeth worked on four years ago. You ought to take her out there to see how well it faired."

"I'm sure it wasn't just the wall."

"Well, it was a low grass fire and I think the wall helped."

Wilbur said, "Sometimes walls can be helpful. We'll go take a look."

The Watsons were sitting on Claude's front porch as Wilbur and Elizabeth approached. Elizabeth immediately strode over to the archway she had helped her father construct and noticed that the roses were untouched by the fire. She surveyed the scorched grassland and shook her head. She had a pretty good idea who and what had caused a near disaster. Off in the distance, she saw smoke drifting up from the lower forest.

Wilbur was listening to the Watsons' account of the previous night's excitement when Elizabeth joined them.

"I'm fairly certain I know how this happened. I'm so sorry. I think some of my classmates were probably involved," said Elizabeth. Elizabeth's sixteenth birthday was not far off and she was already a high school senior. She was also very involved in civic activities and served as the chair of the Bear City Youth Council, responsible for providing teenager perspectives to the mayor and city councilors. She wasn't shy about speaking her mind. When the city proposed an ordinance establishing an under-eighteen 10:00 p.m. curfew for Sunday through Thursday and 11:00 p.m. for Friday and Saturday, she was quick to address the city council stating all the reasons why it "just won't work." Her argument boiled down to her opinion that it was unenforceable and bordered on "silly in this day and age." The city council relented, and Elizabeth gained hero status by those most likely to abuse any restrictions and probably the same incorrigible group who started the grass fire stopped by Wilbur's wall. "I'm going to find out and make sure there are consequences." Elizabeth had an already well-developed sense of justice, which would serve her well as the civil rights attorney she would eventually become.

Like her grandmother, Elizabeth had a few close friends with whom she shared her deepest thoughts and feelings. She also possessed her grandmother's deep listening skills. She had an innate ability to be quiet, show interest, and pick up the slightest nuances when listening to others, especially in uncomfortable situations. She was different than stereotypical adolescents who could be impetuous and quick to jump to judgements and conclusions. Elizabeth pondered. Elizabeth considered various points of view before drawing conclusions.

During the weeks before going back to school, she helped her father build another wall, fished as much as possible with her mother in the river that ran along their property, and met her close friends at Pop's while enjoying a thick vanilla milkshake and, when feeling extravagant, sharing a plate of fries. It was at Pop's, while sitting with her friend Mindy, when she heard Leon Jr., Jeff and Karen at a nearby booth talking about the fire. She thought, "Kids. Kids are either bragging in person or bragging with selfies. Dumb." There were no selfies taken but there was a lot of sharing about how "stupid we were that night." Elizabeth listened. Elizabeth made mental notes. Elizabeth was forming a plan.

Wilbur and Sam were both standing by the river holding hands when Elizabeth arrived home. She loved the affection her parents showed one another. When Elizabeth was in middle school, where Sam was a science teacher, she often overheard other students complaining about their parents. Usually, it was about strife and ongoing conflicts and often about how embarrassing it was when their parents were overly affectionate in public. Elizabeth thought of her parents as smart and cute.

Elizabeth walked toward her parents and quipped, "Fishing or kissing?"

Wilbur and Sam turned, and her mother replied, "A little of both."

"Well, I need to interrupt your quiet time and talk to you about a problem."

Wilbur had built a small fire pit at the river's edge encircled by eight Adirondack chairs. During the summer they would gather after dinner to roast marshmallows and make smores, often with their extended family of Sal, Sally, Lori and Hiram. It was a place to unwind, tell stories, and enjoy each other's company. Now they sat while Wilbur and Sam patiently waited for their daughter to share her concern.

"I've been threatened," said Elizabeth. She went on to explain what she and Mindy had overheard at Pop's. "Leon Jr. told me to keep my mouth shut or I'd pay." Wilbur and Sam continued listening with the confidence of parents who know that their daughter probably had a solution in mind. Elizabeth was not one to be intimidated. However, Leon Jr. presented a challenge different from a stereotypical bully. Leon Jr. had a reputation for intimidating others and a father who would never accept the fact that his son was a bully. Leon's father Leon Sr. was the mayor. Leon Sr. and Leon Jr. were both big. They stood well over six feet and were built like overweight mud wrestlers. The only way to persuade the mayor was by threatening to vote for someone else. The mayor had a reputation for supporting the last person who had access. Yet, he still got elected year after year probably because he was an ingratiating pleaser. He persuaded others to support him by being agreeable to a fault and helping folks maneuver through bureaucracy by virtue of his political position. He benefitted from living in a town with few problems and a lazy electorate. He was not an overt intimidator; rather he was an insidious influencer by exercising his need to be the nice guy. On the other hand, his son was an intimidator. Leon Jr. intimidated with size and bravado. He had a tendency to stride into a room with long, heavy steps demanding attention with just his pure presence. He was also a star football and basketball player, which gave him a touch of high school idolatry. He was an exemplar of high school star power that eventually turns into career failure. His future job security rested in his father's successful hardware store.

"What's your plan?" asked Sam.

"I'm mulling over a few options," said Elizabeth.

Youth Council meetings were always scheduled for the hour preceding the regular Bear City Council meetings. City councilors enjoyed mentoring the Youth Council and proudly sat in the audience like stepparents while the five members of the Youth Council sat in the regular councilors' seats looking down at those in attendance. Usually in attendance were a few other high school students, one or two regulars coming early for the City Council meeting, and the five members of the City Council, which included the mayor. For today's meeting, Elizabeth's parents, as well as her extended family of Sal, Sally, Lori and Hiram, took their places in the back row. Just before Elizabeth called the meeting to order, Wilbur gave a knowing thumbs-up with a broad smile.

The Youth Council had the freedom to develop its own agenda with some direction from the mayor and city councilors. This meeting was scheduled for the week prior to the opening of school and the agenda included a report on the range of summer youth activities sponsored by the city. The councilors anticipated a glowing review of the variety of city-sponsored offerings. A positive description and sincere thank-you is what they heard. Each member of the Youth Council described one sponsored activity along with an account of the number of participants and their ratings based on satisfaction surveys. Elizabeth was the last to report and, rather than describe the week-long backpacking trips into the surrounding wilderness, she announced that she was going to speak to the unauthorized gatherings on the town's outskirts. Before she could elaborate, the mayor interrupted.

"Elizabeth, that's not part of the agenda."

"I know. However, I've spoken with the other members of the Youth Council and we all agree it's important for us to comment on those activities. We feel indebted to bringing up important issues that might have a very bad impact on our city. Wouldn't you agree?"

"Well, of course. It's just that it wasn't on the agenda and we haven't had a chance to mentor you on any new topic.

One of the councilors broke in and suggested that the Youth Council be heard. "I think this is an example of how we want our young people to take responsibility for speaking up. Let's hear what Elizabeth has to say," remarked the councilor.

"Thanks," said Elizabeth. "We all know how the area just outside town and below the forest is a frequent gathering place for teens to party." She went on to describe the recent fire and how she had come to know how it was started. She elaborated how she and her father had gone to the Watson's property the day after the fire began and saw the burn scar first-hand. "It was luck and the Watson's wall that stopped the fire from burning down their residences and moving closer to town. It was three more days before the fire was put out in the forest. And it was all due to a number of my classmates who were acting recklessly. It's something we need to address as an entire community. Wouldn't you agree Mr. Mayor?"

Leon Sr. stood and replied, "Yes, of course." The city councilors nodded in agreement. Elizabeth had set her trap. It wasn't difficult. Leon Sr.'s ego kept him from thinking beyond the moment. His public image was more important than any moral or ethical core he might have. Elizabeth turned to her best friend Mindy, also a member of the Youth Council, and asked her to report on the conversation they had overheard at Pop's and the subsequent threat made by Leon Jr. As she spoke, the mayor's face first reddened and then blanched. The councilors listened with intense seriousness. The entire room frozen in the moment as the horrific story was told matter-of-factly.

After Mindy finished, Elizabeth asked if there were any questions or comments from the councilors. Leon Sr. tried to interrupt but Elizabeth immediately gaveled for quiet and stated that the mayor had a conflict of interest and would not be allowed to comment at that moment.

Sam leaned into Wilbur and whispered, "Our daughter has some good chutzpah. I'm liking this."

Sol, sitting on Wilbur's other side, said, "I'm taking her over to Pop's for a celebratory donut tomorrow morning."

Leon Sr. tried again to make a statement, but Elizabeth again used the power of the gavel to bring the meeting back to order and called upon a councilor who had raised her hand.

"Are you saying the mayor had knowledge of this?"

"No. We don't believe he did. However, we also don't have

confidence that Leon Jr. and the others who were at the party will suffer adequate consequences. And we are prepared to suggest what they ought to be."

With Elizabeth's leadership, the Youth Council presented a plan to the City Council. They wanted Leon Jr. to identify everyone who was at the party where the fire started and require them to attend the next Youth Council meeting. Elizabeth explained that she and another member of the Youth Council would meet with the chief of police and the fire marshal to develop a community service plan requirement for all of the troublemakers to complete in lieu of formal charges being levied. Finally, the Youth Council demanded that Leon Jr. write a formal letter of apology for the group's dangerous misbehavior and his specific threat to Elizabeth and Mindy with the requirement that the letter be read aloud at the next Youth Council meeting 'as a process of allocution."

"Allocution?" asked a city councilor.

"Yes, I've been watching Law and Order," said Elizabeth, which caused a ripple of laughter from the spectators.

Word quickly spread throughout Bear City. Elizabeth began fielding phone calls from a number of high school students thanking her for standing up to Leon Jr. and his friends. School was starting and fall was morphing into full color. The hills surrounding the town bright with various shades of yellow, orange, red, purple, and brown. The municipal park bordering the river springing to life with the season's decay. Wilbur and Sal sat at Pop's early one morning. Wilbur enjoying a mug of black coffee while Sal sipped a macchiato and picked away at a buttermilk bar.

"I heard that Leon Jr. and his friends will be doing forest restoration on the weekends," said Sal. "It seems like an appropriate consequence."

"Yes. But you should have been at the Youth Council meeting when he had to read his letter. The chamber was filled with high school students who were amazingly calm and quiet during the allocution. it was really something when Elizabeth required each of the other dozen or so teens to also apologize aloud."

"I also heard she had something to say about the Watson's wall stopping the fire."

"Well, said Wilbur, "She actually didn't mention that. The Watsons were there as fire victims. Elizabeth had asked them to be present. When the teens finished apologizing, Elizabeth asked the Watsons to respond. It was Mrs. Watson who said something about walls.

"Elizabeth, you worked on our wall with your father. You learned something about how Wilbur's walls can define and protect spaces. I want to thank you for the work you are doing. I think you and the Youth Council are very much like a wall that helps to define the difference between right and wrong."

Richard Makes a Choice

Bear City's population is approximately 28,000 mostly white self-proclaimed progressives who enjoy debating issues without becoming directly involved. As long as the streets are paved, the downtown kept free of chain stores, and the miniscule homeless population kept at bay and fairly invisible, folks are happy with their municipal government. The Mayor and city councilors generally run unopposed and have been in office for longer than most can remember. Unlike the other towns in its region, Bear City's minority populations are tiny and viewed as insignificant. It's a peaceful town that relishes its quaintness and values the small liberal arts university that seamlessly integrates into the town's life and geography. Town officials and university professors eschew titles and kindergarten students call their teachers by their first names.

Few significant issues challenge Bear City leaders. The placement of a new city park took almost six months of open hearings with the pro- and anti-lawn factions engaging in a series of heated arguments. The removal of two heritage trees in another park to make way for a new children's play area brought out picketers and bullhorns for several weeks. Eventually the city council relented and found a less-than-satisfactory placement for the play area thus preserving two Raywood ash trees that had probably reached the end of their life expectancy. Ironically, they were toppled by a fierce windstorm demolishing the adjacent and abandoned-for-safety's-sake park office. Then there was the case of Richard Ellison, one of the few Black residents, who accused the owners of Pop's Donuts and Coffee with discrimination when they did not rehire him for summer employment. The news of Richard's situation caused the city council to instruct the Mayor to approach Hiram Bloom, a well-known philosophy professor, to become the first Bear City Ethics Administrator charged with examining city ordinances, rules and regulations for discriminatory practices while also tasked with beginning a community dialogue focused on equity issues.

Hiram formed the Speak Your Truth Listening Panel where residents representing the town's minority populations were encouraged to tell their stories of discrimination and prejudice. Hiram did not define minorities. He thought it best to allow citizens the opportunity to define it for themselves. As it turned out, those who stepped forward to tell their stories were mostly people of color and members of a larger-than-known LGBTQ community. There were also several left-handed individuals, two circus performers, a mime, and members of the local Overeaters

Anonymous Club.

Hiram intentionally invited the town's most economically powerful citizens to be members of the five-person Panel. When asked by the city councilors why he had chosen the wealthiest white men, he said that it was an opportunity to "speak truth to power." The councilors nodded with an oh-I'm-a-liberal-and-I-get-it expression while the Mayor appeared to fidget. The Mayor asked why the Panel was only allowed to listen, ask probing questions and refrain from making statements. Hiram looked at the Mayor, held a steady gaze, and told him the Panel's duty was to learn and not instruct.

"What we truly hear will help us to form future actions. How we listen will help to heal the wounds of prejudice," said Hiram. "This is not about us needing to be understood. It's about us needing to understand."

Richard was the first to speak. The Panel occupied the councilor's seats looking down on the audience. A blond, highly waxed oak table facing the raised curvilinear platform was reserved for the storyteller. It was very much like a typical hearing room with officials at the front looming over a testifier at a table with other participants and spectators seated in the rear. Richard confidently approached the table. He was twenty-one years old, dressed in his Sunday-best charcoal suit with starched white shirt and bright multi-colored paisley tie, his hair neatly trimmed into a short Afro, he stood without any notes in hand and, before sitting on the hard wooden chair reserved for the speaker, calmly addressed the panel.

"Thank you for doing this. It's long past time to hear from those of us who have quietly endured what I hope you never intended. But before I talk about that, I want to point out that by using this physical structure you are continuing to perpetuate the power structure you seek to address."

Hiram immediately called a break in the proceedings and asked the town's custodian assigned to the meeting to remove the speaker's table, bring in additional chairs like the one Richard was about to use and arrange the chairs in a circle on the chamber's floor.

"Richard, thank you for pointing out our first mistake. Let's continue on as much of an equal footing as possible," said Hiram.

Richard spoke with a voice far exceeding his youth. He described how growing up in Bear City helped him to develop an intellectual drive in the context of separateness. He enumerated examples of being called on by his teachers more often than his white classmates in elementary, middle and high school classes.

"I believe my teachers' intentions were good. They wanted me to feel included. They actually caused me to be exceptionally well-prepared because I knew early on, I would be called on much more than in a random fashion. The reality was that I was called on more often because I look different. If you were to ask my former teachers, they would probably say they didn't see color. But they did. In fact, I think that's okay. It's ludicrous to think we don't see difference. In my case, it caused me to be a better student. However, more often than not, it doesn't. I am fortunate to have parents who brought me up as a reader, exposed me to a variety of cultural activities, didn't allow me to watch too much television or play video games, and insisted on conversations around the dinner table. Every student brings their own unique culture to school and teachers need to be interested in each of us as unique students."

Richard went on to talk about times when he was asked to be "representative of his people" and give a personal perspective of the Civil Rights Movement. "It was before I was even born. It's more a part of my grandparents' history. And I'm asked to be an expert. Singling me out was insulting." He also emphasized that he never thought of his teachers as mean-spirited or unhelpful. He recounted several teachers that taught him to be a better writer and more curious about history and current events. He specifically talked about his middle school science teacher who taught him about the scientific method and instilled in him inquisitiveness about the natural world.

While Richard spoke, the Mayor sat in the back of the room arms crossed wondering what Richard's problem was. It sounded that he had a wonderful school experience. He received all kinds of special attention. Why would he complain about that? He was an exceptional student who came from a family that was esteemed and honored by the Chamber of Commerce. He appeared to have all the privileges enjoyed by any other Bear City family. He thought about when Richard didn't get rehired at Pop's, but that was a special situation regarding a promise made to the former owners of the café. Besides, it all worked out when the owner of Moshe's Deli stepped in to help fund the continuation of Richard's job. Where was the problem? Bear City took good care of its own.

Richard paused for a moment and a Panel member took the opportunity to ask a question, "I'm curious, Mr. Ellison, about the discrimination you experienced in school. It sounds like you received a lot of extra attention and support and did well enough to go on to a select university. How did you experience prejudice?"

Richard scanned the Panel noticing the seriousness of the five white men. The panelists appeared a bit uneasy sitting without the security of an elevated platform and the barrier of the curved counselor's bench. Hiram sat directly across from Richard with much more ease and self-assuredness. He and Richard had spoken a number of weeks earlier about the Panel's goal to listen and understand. At one point in their conversation, Richard shared that he didn't think he would be the best to talk about discrimination. "After all, Professor Bloom, I'm a success story. I don't think others will view my success as an example of prejudice." It was when Hiram asked Richard to walk with him around town and reflect on what he saw.

"Look inward and outward, Richard. Think about the bigger pitcher while living the smaller one," suggested Hiram.

Richard recalled the time he applied to be a member of the Youth Council. He submitted his application to the City Council and was informed that he would not be selected. When he asked why he was rejected, he was told that he didn't have any previous involvement in youth activities and lacked the necessary experience required of Youth Council members.

Richard responded to the Panel members question, "It's not just about me. There are members of our community who experience constant separateness." Richard asked the Panel to look at each other and ask themselves who they represented. "Look at the City Council. Look at the police and fire departments. Look at the schools, the university, the service clubs, the downtown shop owners, look around at all the public organizations and businesses. With the exception of my parents' store, which is not located downtown, where do you see people of color, women, and other minority groups in positions that influence life in our town? After I finish, you'll hear stories by those who have faced individual discrimination. I touched a bit on that, but I wanted you to see a larger picture. One about the lack of interconnectedness that we need to overcome".

After Richard concluded, Hiram called for a fifteen-minute recess. Richard turned to leave, and the Mayor stood before him. Leon Sr., all six-foot plus and mid-200 pounds, a sheen of sweat around his tight collar, showing a closed-lipped smile and extending his hand, which Richard shook while sensing a bit of clammy nervousness in the Mayor.

"Nice job, Richard. I hope the other speakers tell their story as well as you. You are certainly an asset for our wonderful town."

"Thanks, Mayor. I trust you listened as well as the Panel," replied Richard and he strode from the room.

Outside the hearing room, Wilbur and Sal met Richard and asked if he'd like to join them at Pop's for coffee and a bit of decompression conversation. Richard asked if they had been in the room and Wilbur said they listened over the speakers while sitting in the hallway.

Sal said, "Impressive testimony, Richard. I learned a lot. I want to hear more of your story. You know, lately I've been deconstructing flowers and rearranging their parts before photographing them. It's not unlike your story, which might help to deconstruct a bit of life around here and suggest ways of reconstructing new patterns of connectedness. Very impressive, indeed."

Richard smiled, "Sal, I thought Hiram was the only real philosopher in town."

When they walked into Pop's, Phyllis ran over and hugged Richard. She told him about a number of phone calls she had already received extolling Richard's appearance. Word travelled fast in Bear City and often straight through Pop's.

"Coffee and treats are on Jack and me today." From behind the counter, Jack gave a double thumbs up. Phyllis served Sal an espresso and cherry turnover. Wilbur had his usual black coffee and Richard asked for a lime Italian soda without whipped cream. At Richard's urging, Phyllis and Jack had recently put fancy sodas on the menu and offered a dozen different flavored syrups. They had already become big sellers with the afterschool teenage crowd.

Sal took a bite of his turnover, "Phyllis and Jack keep making Pop's better and better. I remember when you could only get black coffee with a slightly fresh donut or a fairly good egg salad sandwich for lunch. I think Moshe's Deli has helped them to up their game."

Richard smiled, "Diversity ups everyone's game."

"When are you planning to run for office? You've got the gift," said Sal.

Before Richard could reply, Wilbur mentioned that the City Council had asked him to build a wall to enclose a new city rose garden. Sal would be in charge of selecting and planting a variety of roses.

"I'm thinking of a different kind of wall," said Wilbur.

On the day of the wall and garden dedication, Wilbur and Sal stood with Richard and his parents Mr. and Mrs. Ellison. The spectators included the Mayor, city councilors, Hiram and his wife Lori, Wilbur's wife Sam and their daughter Elizabeth, Sal's wife Sally, and the thirty-three other storytellers who had addressed the Speak Your Truth Listening Panel. It was a bright, sunny day. The sort of day that invites "how-are-you" passing conversations. A day made for congratulations and encouragement. Wilbur and Sal had asked Richard to be the event's speaker. The wall and garden were intended to be representative of the Panel's summary report.

Richard stood without any notes before the assembled group, wearing his Sunday-best charcoal suit with starched white shirt and bright multi-colored paisley tie, his hair neatly trimmed into a medium-length Afro. He had recently graduated with a degree in business administration and was now working in his family's specialty market developing a plan for expansion and the possibility of franchising the store. He stood straight and quiet, waiting for the crowd to focus on him. He did not need to verbally call attention; his presence was enough.

"This is a special wall and garden," he began with a clear, baritone voice. "You'll notice that Wilbur built what he calls a 'deconstructed wall.' While the stones create a border, they do so in what appears to be in a random fashion. Yet, that randomness manages to contain the beauty of a diverse collection of gorgeous roses in a very unique way. Wilbur and Sal want us to appreciate the potential of the monumental work accomplished by Hiram and the Panel. I am proud to stand before you today to dedicate this wall and garden as one step forward in the shared pursuit of a more inclusive community. As a result of the Panel's report, changes have already begun. We now have new leadership more representative of our town in many appointed city positions. Service clubs and other voluntary organizations have begun to actively recruit members reflecting our town's diversity. Now, it's time to diversify elected positions. That is why I'm here to honor this accomplishment and also announce that I will be running for mayor in the upcoming election."

Sally Learns to Paint

There's a time during each fall morning when orange light illuminates a flower's colors in such a way that they seem almost translucent and something more than just a blossom. It's as though there is an inner life. For those fortunate enough to be awake and outdoors at that time, it can be both inspiring and mystifying. Sally once described it as an awakening from sleep's pause button.

Artists seek those precious seconds. For Sally, just before turning thirteen, it was when she became a watercolorist. It's when she painted a white rose's leaf that showed precision and a sense of inner illumination. It's when Sally began a lifelong love affair with painting flowers using the whims and fancies of watercolors.

Sally grew up in Santa Fe, New Mexico in a middle-class family where her parents owned a small, well-respected art gallery situated below their cozy two-bedroom apartment. There was always a corner in the gallery and the apartment set up with art supplies where, as a young child, Sally would spend hours fingerpainting and discovering how colors interacted with one another. As she grew up, she used popsicle sticks and brushes to paint more controlled pictures. Her elementary teachers often exhibited her pictures on the school's public bulletin boards and encouraged her burgeoning talent. Although Santa Fe was an arts town with many children emulating their artist parents, Sally quickly stood out as one not trying to merely emulate what she saw at home, but as a young person with her own style and artistic eye. When she was in third grade, her teacher described her talent at a parent-teacher conference in soccer terms.

"If you watch a soccer game, you'll often notice that one player stands out among all the others with a different level of grace and skill. That's the way Sally is with art."

Sally's parents didn't like the athletic analogy. They didn't see art as a competition. They encouraged Sally but didn't make demands. They often took her to other galleries and museums, and it was when Sally saw her first Georgia O'Keeffe flower paintings that she felt the pull to become a professional artist. Shortly thereafter and just before Sally turned thirteen, her parents took her to Kauai for a two-week vacation. That was when she met one of the island's Living Treasures.

Sylvia Kato-Eisenberg, commonly known as Mother Sylvie, was an esteemed watercolorist who had once studied with the great O'Keeffe. Now in her mid-80's, she had recently been honored as a Living Treasure along with Auntie Esther, a legendary weaver of hats made from native palm fronds. It just so happened that both Mother Sylvie and Auntie Esther were being celebrated by the Kauai Museum with exhibitions of their work as well as demonstrations of their art.

Mother Sylvie was seated at a card table with a beginner's Winsor & Newton Cotman watercolor set, two jars of water and a Strathmore pad of paper when Sally approached and stood before her. Mother Sylvie had just begun painting an Anthurium. Sally's parents had already moved to other parts of the museum while Sally quietly observed Mother Sylvie mixing color and confidently brushing layers of color onto her artist's pad. The red flower beginning to bloom with deep, enamel-like color.

Fifteen minutes passed before Mother Sylvie asked, "Are you a painter?"

"I have a set of watercolors and I try," answered Sally.

Mother Sylvie nodded and asked, "What problems are you working on?"

Sally was stunned. She wondered why this tiny, gray-haired woman with dark eyes shimmering with curiosity would ask such a question. Here she was standing before a Living Treasure who seemed to be putting her on an equal artistic footing.

"I'm sorry Ms. Kato-Eisenberg, I'm not really an artist," replied Sally.

"How can you be so sure? And, please, call me Mother Sylvie."

"I'm just a kid. You're a real artist."

Mother Sylvie set her brush aside and looked up at Sally. She remembered when her late husband Max Eisenberg, a holocaust survivor who made his fortune with a string of franchised bagel shops, suggested they travel to Santa Fe so that she could meet and study with Georgia O'Keeffe. Having grown up Japanese American, she survived her own internment when her family was confined to the Hood River relocation camp during World War II. After the war, she met Max while attending art school in New York City. Max had just opened his first bagel shop and was behind the counter when Sylvia entered and looked over the four different types of bagels Max offered: plain, poppy, sesame and onion. As Max grew the business into a thriving empire, there would eventually be over twenty varieties available with a wide selection of schmears. Sylvia ordered a plain bagel with cream cheese and discovered she had left her coin purse back at her apartment. Max told her not to worry and even treated her to a cup of coffee. Sylvia sat at a small round table by the front window. She was the only patron and Max came over to warm her coffee and begin a conversation that lasted his lifetime. After Max's passing, Sylvia sold their New York condominium and moved to their second home in Kauai where she quickly became Mother Sylvie the Living Treasure and master of floral watercolors.

With her soft, gentle voice, Mother Sylvie said, "You're young and will develop your skills and techniques. That takes time, discipline and commitment. Being an artist is not about craft. It's about heart, empathy, and a unique point-of-view. Come, sit next to me and show me how you'd paint this flower. I'll share my set with you."

For the next two hours, Sally quietly painted alongside Mother Sylvie. Sally's parents walked by several times without interrupting. Sally was so focused, she never noticed them. Sally paused and asked Mother Sylvie when she knew she was finished.

"That's a good question. When is a flower finished growing? Yes, they eventually begin to decay, but then their remains help to nourish future blooms. As painters, we can only capture moments. I'll be painting this flower for the next two weeks. Each day I'll turn the flower a bit to capture another view. I'll try my best to know this Anthurium from the inside out. If you'd like, and if your parents allow, we could work on this together."

For the remainder of her vacation, Sally's parents dropped her off at the museum each morning so that she could paint with Mother Sylvie. Auntie Esther stopped at the table one day to comment that one Living Treasure was in the process of mentoring another. She observed the two artists for a few minutes before leaving and returning with a gift for Sally.

"I'd like you to have one of my hats. You've earned it."

Sally wore the handwoven hat with her usual T-shirt, shorts and flip-flops every day. Her parents commented that packing for the trip would have been much easier if they knew her wardrobe was going to be so simple. Then, again, they didn't have any way of predicting that she would have the opportunity and privilege of painting with Mother Sylvie every day. Toward the end of their vacation, Sally's parents convinced Mother Sylvie to join them for dinner at a restaurant of her choice. She suggested that meet at the Hanapepe Café.

"I live in Hanapepe. It's our island's art colony and the café is an institution. It's more of a bakery, but they serve Italian dinners on Friday night. I hope you don't mind vegetarian. For dessert, they make a macadamia nut crème brulee worth the drive."

The café didn't take reservations, but Mother Sylvie was already seated at a table covered by a freshly laundered white linen tablecloth and set with upscale silver plate cutlery. The walls were filled with a collection of local artists' paintings, including several by Mother Sylvie. Notable was the first version of the Anthurium Sally had watched Mother Sylvie paint.

They were enjoying their desserts when Mother Sylvie said she was looking forward to painting with Sally in the morning. Sally's parents reminded Mother Sylvie and Sally that they would be flying home on Sunday and asked if Sally wanted to spend her last day painting.

"Of course, I have so much more to learn. And don't worry, this has been the best vacation ever."

Before leaving the café, Mother Sylvie nodded to the cashier who took down the Anthurium painting and brought it to the table. Mother Sylvie stood, took the painting, turned and handed it to Sally. "I want you to have this painting. You've worked hard for almost two weeks and I'm very proud of the work you are doing."

"But Mother Sylvie, you said you never sell your paintings. You said you keep all the originals and only sell prints."

"I'm not selling you a painting. It's a gift. You have a special talent. I hope you'll send me one of your paintings someday. I would be honored to have one."

Sally rose, a head taller than Mother Sylvie, placed the painting on her chair and threw her arms around Mother Sylvie. "I don't know how to possibly thank you. You've done so much for me already. This is so special."

Their last day together was a mix of joy, sadness and intense learning. Sally had so many questions that extended well beyond her age.

"What should I pay the most attention to?" asked Sally.

"It's not about the 'most.' However, you also need to notice the empty spaces. You will learn how to leave something unpainted. Consider the space outside what you are painting."

"I'm trying hard to copy what you are doing, but I can't seem to get it just right."

"Mimicry is flattering, Sally. However, if my work causes you to find something original…if I can inspire…then I'll be honored."

Mother Sylvie's responses always included a 'however.' She was complimentary and always extending and pushing Sally to see herself as an artist. She had come to recognize Sally's innate gift and encouraged her to trust her own instincts.

At one point Sally remarked, "The veining is so hard to get right."

"Now you are finding interesting problems. Remember when I asked what problems you were having. It's all part of the process. A constant problem for me is learning to use water's transparency and less about trying to overcome water's nature with color. There will always be problems and we can only hope they are interesting ones."

In less than two weeks, Sally and Mother Sylvie had learned to communicate in the unique language of watercolorists. Sally returned home with a portfolio of her Anthurium paintings, and the one Mother Sylvie had given her.

Sally was committed to an artist's life. She was motivated to excel in school and gain admittance to a prestigious college where she graduated with bachelor's and master's degrees in art. She also managed to earn a teaching credential, but she left teaching after a few years. She was never comfortable with prescribed routines and was fascinated and respectful of her colleagues who were able to work within the rules. Mostly, she enjoyed working with middle schoolers, as it brought back fond memories of her time with Mother Sylvie. She especially valued sitting side-by-side with those students who asked for more attention. She found herself summoning many of the same questions Mother Sylvie had posed.

As she began to gain some notoriety as a fine watercolorist, the sale of her paintings afforded her the opportunity to give up the security of a regular paycheck. She thought more and more about Mother Sylvie's notion about not selling her original work. Sally believed that mass producing her paintings would ultimately reduce the value of her originals and she took great pride in the personal relationships she developed with her patrons. Unlike Mother Sylvie, she took joy in selling her paintings, especially to those who became close friends. It was one of those friendships with Eli and her son Wilbur that led to her meeting and marrying Sal.

It had been nearly seventy years since Sally met and worked with Mother Sylvie. She and Sal share a small studio Sal built in their backyard and situated in a lush garden of flowers and deciduous trees. They both enjoyed marking the seasons with a tree's visible life cycle and a flowers' seasonal blooms. Her latest project has been to paint all the flowers within a 100-mile radius of Bear City while Sal works at taking pictures of those same flowers as newly arranged deconstructed versions.

Although Sally had kept in frequent touch with Mother Sylvie until her peaceful passing from old age, she had never returned to the island. The Kauai Museum invited Sally to spend a month as an artist-in-residence and she couldn't resist the offer to paint again and feel Mother

Sylvie's wisdom and presence. She hoped she might even have a chance to inspire a young painter, as Mother Sylvie had done for her. She spent the first week painting a red Anthurium. The museum director, who knew of the special relationship between Sally and Mother Sylvie, publicized Sally's residency as a return of an Honorary Living Treasure. Sally painted for four hours each day and then she and Sal enjoyed poking around the island like any other tourist. Sally especially enjoyed taking Sal to the Hanapepe Café where she retold the story of dinner with Mother Sylvie and the gift of the Anthurium painting which hung in their art studio back home.

Wilbur and his wife Sam were close friends. While Sally and Sal were in Kauai, Wilbur designed and built a low wall around their art studio, which Sally and Sal discovered after returning from Kauai. It was planted with native Hawaiian flowers and the large stone forming a corner where the steps led to the front door was etched "Sally—Bear City Living Legend."

Sally and Sal stood holding hands and admiring the wall. Wilbur, who had been waiting in the studio for their arrival home, opened the door, walked into the yard and asked, "How do you like your anniversary present?"

Sal said, "You have a way with walls."

More Stories

Abby Learns to Play the Tuba

There's that look my poodle gives when I ask her a question. "Emmy, would you like to solve a math problem? Emmy, what do you think of the current state of politics in our town?" She cocks her head in a way that I suppose all dogs...smart ones like poodles...do when faced with an inquiry that doesn't involve going for a walk. It's the same look my wife gave me when I asked, "Abby, what do you think about the two of us taking tuba lessons?"

"Huh?"

"It would be something we could do together. It might be fun."

Abby and I have been married for seventeen years. We chose to never have children and live our lives filled with adventure and unpredictability. We met shortly after graduating from college, filled with ideals and the visions of perfection, with good jobs, and a passion for each other. We tried to break out of any perceived ruts by signing up for painting, dancing... tango was a disaster...and music appreciation classes. We took vacations that family members questioned: studying fire ants in Texas, archeological digs in Cambodia...watching out for land mines...and adult space camp in Alabama. Neither of us played any musical instruments.

"But we're not musical. And why tuba?"

"I thought we could do Oktoberfest in Germany and join an oompah band."

"Seriously?"

"Why not?"

We found Helga's Top Brass Music by Googling tuba lessons. The website said that they had instruments and lessons for every age group. We entered and noticed an older gentleman behind the counter. He was a stout fellow and sported an immense gray beard. He greeted us and asked how he might be of assistance.

Abby said, "We called about tuba lessons."

He looked us over with an amused expression. Abby is the definition of cute and petite; I am sturdy and small. I had the sense that he didn't see us as hefty enough to play a large brass instrument, much less lug it around.

"Might I interest you in a trumpet or perhaps a French horn. Tubas are quite large and heavy."

"No, we are determined to learn how to play the tuba," replied Abby. I had always admired Abby's assertiveness once she made up her mind. When I first broached the idea of tuba lessons, her first response after "seriously?" was to think about it. Less than a few hours later, she proclaimed, "Find us some tubas and an instructor. We're going to Oktoberfest in two years."

As it turns out Helga was Otto's mother. She was retired, and Otto had taken over the family business. For the first year of our lessons, he insisted that we learn while remaining seated. We slowly moved beyond what he termed "initial instrument farts," while learning to read simple music notation and making progress into the tuba's deep, sonorous noises and then recognizable sounds. Abby was a quick learner and began making decipherable sounds early on. It took me months before I was able to match the noise with the musical notations. Otto often scratched his wiry head of graying hair in wonderment of Abby's ability to blow enough air through the tuba's mouthpiece. My breathing was consistently too shallow, my lips either too tense or too lax, and my fingering uncontrollable. Otto would utter, "Abby, you're getting to oompah, but your husband is barely at oomph!"

On a rainy December evening, a little over a year since we began our lessons, Abby asked me if I thought we'd be ready to play publicly at the next Oktoberfest. "Abby, I think you are well on your way. You have real tuba talent. I'm not sure about myself." I had begun to grasp the idea that my musical talent might be as a listener and not as a player. Yet, giving up was not part of my personality.

"Maybe tuba is not your thing. Let's ask Otto."

At our next lesson, we talked with Otto about options. Knowing that oompah bands typically employ trumpets, trombones, clarinets, tubas, accordions, and drummers, he suggested I take up the tambourine or cowbell. "It would be unusual but refreshing."

The switch to a rhythmic instrument was not easy. It turns out my weak breaths and fumbling fingers on the tuba were not my only musical shortcomings. Apparently, I lacked a basic sense of rhythm. Otto convinced me that playing a simple woodblock was my calling. For the next year, Abby and I rehearsed daily. Otto described the sounds emanating from her tuba playing as, "round, robust, earthy, and resonant." To me he said, "You are mostly in rhythm, but be gentler with the hammer on the block."

September arrived and Abby had learned several typical Oktoberfest songs. She was confident that she could play simple tunes with an oompah band. What was even more amazing was that Otto believed she had a highly tuned ear and could improvise even when she didn't know the song. "You're a natural, Abby."

Our plan was to fly to Munich and participate in the festivities by spontaneously joining bands at one of the many so-called pop-up events. We figured that there would be enough beer being hoisted and sausages consumed to keep others from paying much attention to us.

Oktoberfest felt like Mardi Gras with lederhosen. We checked into our hotel carrying only backpacks and one tuba. My woodblock fit easily into my backpack. The front desk clerk welcomed us with a broad grin… probably reserved for Americans… and a guide to Munich's celebratory activities. After a short in-room rehearsal, we were interrupted by a call from the front desk asking us to be respectful of neighboring guests. Abby wiped down her recently purchased tuba treating it like an infant. I left my woodblock on the chair. We went in search of a quiet place for dinner. The front desk clerk suggested a small delicatessen off the beaten track. "You won't find any revelers there, and the food is moderately priced and very good."

The hotel was amazingly quiet, and we both slept well in spite of the time change. Abby suggested we take a walk and get our bearings, find a place for breakfast, and ask locals where we might want to go for good local oompah music. One thing we found early on was that our inability to speak German was not a barrier to communication. Every German we encountered spoke excellent English.

"You want to hear oompah?"

"Actually, we came to play."

"Oh, what instruments do you play?"

"I play tuba, my husband woodblock."

"Woodblock? There are no woodblocks in oompah bands."

Later that evening, when festivities were liveliest, Abby carried her tuba and I my not-an-oompah-band woodblock. We returned to a rustic square we had noticed earlier in the day. It was set up with long tables and filled with revelers. We were immediately welcomed by a young woman wearing a traditional dirndl. She recognized us as Americans and asked in her unaccented English, "You are here with the band? The rest of your group will arrive shortly. Sit and I'll bring you steins." Then she glanced at the woodblock and added, "I suppose you'll be watching and listening while your lady friend plays."

Now I was determined to make my woodblock sing. I kept hearing Otto's voice, "Hold your instrument like a butterfly, feel it's beautiful wings flapping, and allow rich tones to escape."

The musicians arrived and began playing recognizable Volksmusik that Otto had prepared us for. Abby and I edged behind and joined in. Abby had no problem picking up the rhythms and effortlessly blended in. Several of the band members turned their heads toward Abby smiling with their eyes and nodding approval. At the end of the first song, the other tuba player welcomed Abby with a pat on the back. "You play well for a tiny girl. Please, continue." Then he turned to me, "There are no percussion instruments like yours in our band, so please enjoy the music from the bench. Also, you still need to work on your rhythm."

I smiled at Abby and encouraged her to continue. I was benched just like when I tried out for Little League baseball. The band played a dozen or so songs and then strutted off while continuing to play. Abby marched with them. I trailed behind having left my woodblock behind.

When we returned to our hotel room, Abby was ecstatic. She had triumphed and could feel it in her entire being. While I knew I was a failed musician, I was proud of her. She wiped off her tuba and gently set it back in its case. She tenderly embraced me and whispered in my ear, "I am the tuba."

Grand Piano

Ivan lives in a neighborhood of grand pianos. It's not a community of grand homes; rather, more of a collection of modest, well-kept houses with well-maintained lawns and comfortably furnished front porches along tree-lined streets. It seems like every other house has a grand piano, but there are just a dozen or so pianos in the neighborhood with a couple being grand. One of the pianos once belonged to his deceased wife Isabel who insisted that it be given to the girl down the block, once one of Isabel's beginning piano students. "She plays that dreadful upright and I want her to have my Steinway if I should die while she's still living at home." Shortly after Ivan's wife died from an unexpected stroke while undergoing cancer treatment, Ivan gave the then 14-year-old Cynthia the polished, perfectly tuned, and eloquently played grand piano.

When Ivan takes his morning and evening walks, he hears music along the way. Wonderful music played by older and younger folks. The older pianists play with the comfort of years at the keyboard. The younger players continue to take lessons and from them there is a range of tentative noise to growing fluidity. Ivan can tell the difference between those who will quit, the ones who will gain a lifetime skill that allows them to entertain guests at house parties, and those who have a musical gift. Ivan enjoys pausing in front of those homes where Chopin, Debussy, or Schubert fill the air with classical mastery. He even has permission to sit on many of the front porches and listen as long as he'd like. Ivan lives in a musical anomaly.

Ivan's own experiences with learning several instruments began in the fourth grade with violin lessons. He played well enough to join the community youth orchestra in junior high school but wasn't a happy violinist. In high school, he switched to the upright bass and enjoyed playing in a small jazz band with friends. He became a self-taught guitarist in college and found himself immersed in the Sixties folk music scene and playing with a garage band two or three times a week. He never tried playing the piano, although after his wife's passing, found great comfort from Horowitz, Gould, and Rubenstein. Now, deep into his senior years, he's become an appreciative listener.

Ivan spends much of his time sitting on the Berkowitz's front porch listening to sixteen-year-old daughter Cynthia playing his dead wife's Steinway with great virtuosity. When Isabel declared that Cynthia needed a more skillful teacher, she auditioned and became a homeschooled protégé of Dr. Gregor Vladimir Semenov, a professor at the local university and world-renowned pianist who mentors two or three musicians whom he says possess the "Gift of Orpheus." He began working with Cynthia when she was eleven years old, well before she was gifted Isabel's Steinway. That was when Professor Semenov declared that "the piano was like having a pair of new hands." For the last two years, Cynthia has fully embraced the professor's instruction and has been committed to becoming a preeminent musician with dreams of playing with the world's greatest orchestras before packed houses of adoring fans. Cynthia had developed a slight case of grandiosity much like many teenagers with prodigious talent.

On this particular Thursday morning, Ivan sat on the Berkowitz's front porch after having completed his regular morning walk where he heard music from three different pianos along the way. There was a haltingly played Scriabin sonata obviously being practiced by a struggling player; a pretty Bach prelude performed with a deftness he hadn't heard from that house before; and another Bach prelude that wasn't so pretty. Perhaps the two Bach players were taking lessons from the same teacher, but clearly not from Dr. Semenov. Cynthia was his only student in this neighborhood, and currently one of the few protégés under the great teacher's tutelage.

Ivan is seventy-nine and in good shape from all his walking around. He has a bit of a paunch that only shows when he sits, as it did now while sitting on one of the cushioned wicker chairs while waiting to hear Cynthia play. At that moment it was quiet, and Ivan admired the yellow roses bordering the front porch. Dr. Semenov pulled up to curb in his nondescript and older Honda Accord, exited, and walked up the front pathway.

"Good morning, professor."

"Nice to see you, Ivan."

"What will Cynthia be practicing today?"

"She is insistent on playing Chopin."

"Wonderful," said Ivan. "I will certainly enjoy my porch listening this morning."

The front door opened, and Cynthia stepped out. "Good morning, Dr. Semenov. Hi, Ivan. Would you like to come inside and listen?"

"No, no, I'll just sit here. I'm looking forward to Chopin."

While Ivan was not a short person, Cynthia towered over him. In Ivan's eyes, she could have been a supermodel with her height and beauty if she hadn't chosen the piano. She exuded a confidence, poise and intellect that could take her in whatever direction she chose.

"Well, you are always welcome to listen inside anytime you'd like," replied Cynthia.

"Cynthia will be working on a nocturne today, Ivan. I'm sure you'll enjoy it and I'm guessing you'll find it a familiar piece," remarked Dr. Semenov.

After the front door was shut, Ivan began talking to his wife. "Izzy, she plays so well. She's almost as good as you were."

"I knew she would be. She will pass me by in no time."

"You were the best. I'm only just now getting the music back."

"Don't let it go, Ivan. And don't get in the way of Cynthia's dreams."

Then Ivan heard the first of Chopin's singular notes being played by Cynthia. He closed his eyes and put his wife's voice aside while listening to Cynthia play a few bars and pause so that Professor Semenov could comment before she replayed the same part with a noticeable shift in technique and emotion. The nocturne became a tad slower and more introverted. Cynthia was finding her own meaning in a seemingly simple piece of music. Ivan recalled the darkness that came over Isabel whenever she played the nocturnes evoking the evening's darker hues. She would sit at the piano and lose herself in the mood, but, when finished, would open her eyes with a renewed sense of insight into her own relationship with Ivan.

"Ivan, the nocturnes bring me closer to you. Each one tells me a story of a quiet journey without words filled with love and tenderness."

Early in their almost fifty-year marriage, Isabel wanted to take her music to wider audiences. She had developed a reputation in their own community performing at small venues. She had placed high in a number of prestigious piano competitions and had won a few less important ones. Several agents had approached her with offers of record contracts and potential tours. However, Ivan was concerned that a career as a performing artist might damage their marriage and plans for a family. He convinced Isabel to focus on teaching and local performances. Ivan's gentle persuasion was effective. Isabel also wanted to start a family and knew that travel could make family life difficult. It was a different society at the beginning of their marriage than at the end. As it turned out, their two daughters both grew up to become self-assured women who managed careers and home life with much greater equity than Ivan's and Isabel's. Ivan marveled at their daughters' success. Isabel felt an emptiness because of it.

"Izzy, the girls are doing very well. Their lives seem to get busier and busier; they still call me often to ask how I'm doing and also tell me how much they miss you. It's been two years, and you are very, very present.

We raised two wonderful daughters, Izzy. You were always there for them. They adore you."

Ivan listened as Cynthia continued to play the nocturne over and over with less pausing and instruction from Dr. Semenov. The notes seemed to be flowing effortlessly with a newfound richness and tone.

"I think the Steinway is in good hands," said Ivan. "Cynthia seems to be an extension of you, Izzy."

"I hope not," replied Isabel with a touch of gratitude and sadness in her quiet voice.

Ivan had been sitting, listening, and talking for little more than an hour when the music stopped, and the front door opened. Out stepped Dr. Semenov and Cynthia.

"You're still here, Ivan," remarked Cynthia. "Is everything okay?"

"Oh, I was caught up in the music today. The nocturnes were so special when Isabel played them. You remind me of her."

Dr. Semenov said, "Your wife was a fine teacher and musician, and I'm so happy she sent Cynthia to me. I'll see you next time, Ivan."

Ivan rose, bid goodbye, and began walking home. Along the way he paused to listen to Malcom Pierce, an eight-year-old beginning piano player, practicing scales on an ancient upright piano that Malcom's parents bought when the elementary school abandoned its music programs and was disposing of all their instruments. Ivan attended numerous school board meetings to plead with the board to keep the diminishing arts programs. He spoke on behalf of his wife, explaining how elementary music programs changed her life and ultimately the lives of others. When a board member asked Ivan if he had grandchildren attending the district schools in deference to his obvious senior status, Ivan replied that his own children had attended the schools but questioned what difference that would make. He talked about the joy he experienced each day when walking around his neighborhood and hearing music flowing from tidy homes and loving families. "Music is the soul of our community," said Ivan with his customary gentleness. "You mustn't take it away." The few parents in the audience applauded Ivan and afterward approached him sharing their gratitude and appreciation.

Ivan smiled as Malcom tentatively maneuvered through his scales and continued his walk home. The cherry tree to the right of his porch was filled with ripening cherries. "Izzy, we're going to have tons of cherries this year if the birds leave us a few. I think I'll make a batch of my grandfather's vishnick this year. You always liked it."

"Oh, Ivan, I liked it for you. There's no reason to keep making it. You'll either throw it out or give it away."

"I paused on my walk home to listen to a young boy playing his scales. You never knew Malcom. I don't think he'll ever be very good, but you never know."

"It's always hard to predict, Ivan. Try not to interfere."

"I'm going to make some lunch. I think I'll call the girls and check in."

When Isabel began teaching their oldest daughter Rachel to play the piano, Ivan would come home from work looking forward to hearing the progress she had made. He would close his eyes, fold his hands under his chin, and listen pensively. When Rachel was ten, she began to show signs of having her mother's gift. Her younger sister Annabel was approaching the age that Isabel thought appropriate for music lessons but showed no interest. "Don't you want to be like your sister Rachel?"

"No."

"You don't want to play the piano, Annabel?"

"No."

Unlike Rachel, Annabel never had an interest in music of any kind. She loved books spent all of her free time reading and going though one series after another, from *Little House on the Prairie* to *Lemony Snicket* and *Harry Potter*. She was destined to become a librarian.

Both of their daughters took their own paths to careers and personal lives. And both had entirely different approaches to music. Rachel stuck with the piano until her late teens when she developed an interest in science and rocketry. She went on to earn a PhD in astrophysics and works at a government-funded think tank on projects she is not allowed to talk about. Rachel has yet to marry or even be in any sort of a serious relationship. Ivan and Isabel could never figure out why she seemed distant and comfortable in being in a world totally separate from theirs. The only change in closing that distance happened after Isabel's death when Rachel began calling her father several times a week.

Ivan thought back to those conversations with Annabel about her firm stand against taking music lessons, which, in retrospect, were tense and demanding even with his soft voice.

"Why don't you want to play the piano, Annabel?"

"Daddy, I don't want to play. Leave me alone."

And that was the way those conversations went. Rachel, on the other hand, simply announced at the dinner table when she was eighteen,

"I quit. I'm done with the piano." Isabel and Ivan stared at one another in disbelief not knowing what to say. Isabel was resigned to the fact that music wasn't for everyone, as she often advised the parents of many of her students who didn't want to stick with piano.

"We mustn't let Rachel give it up so easily," said Ivan.

"Kids go through phases, Ivan. She may come back to it."

Now married, Annabel and her husband Paul live in a nearby town with Ivan's and Isabel's only grandchild Zeke, who recently turned thirteen. Their busy work and family schedules leave little time for visits, which Ivan deeply regrets. He would like a closer relationship with Zeke. Before her death, Isabel spent most after-school afternoons with Zeke.

"What do you do all day with our grandson?" asked Ivan.

"Oh, the usual babysitting activities, Ivan. He gets a snack, does his homework, waits for Annabel to pick him up."

"How about the piano?"

"I won't pressure him, Ivan."

About the time Isabel began taking care of Zeke, she took on a renewed passion for performance. She accepted more local events and told Ivan she wanted to pursue other opportunities. She even thought of contacting an agent to see if there was still any interest in representing her. However, that's when Isabel found the first of several lumps in her breast. Surgery and chemotherapy changed her plans. Her life felt paused and urgent. She once again abandoned her dream and was determined to put all her energies into family, especially Zeke, and recovery.

Ivan made himself his favorite sandwich, tuna and egg salad on rye bread with a dill pickle on the side. He poured himself a club soda and took his lunch out to the back porch with the morning paper he had yet to read. The phone rang and it was Annabel.

"How are you, dad?"

"Just about to eat lunch and then I was going to call you. You beat me to it."

"Should I call back?"

"No, no, this is a good time. I had a very nice walk this morning. The Berkowitz girl is really something. She might be as good as your mother someday."

"That's good, dad. She really appreciates the Steinway. Mom really wanted her to have it."

"A special gift for a special girl."

"Dad, I'm calling about your birthday. You're going to be eighty next month. I spoke to Rachel and she is coming out to help you celebrate."

"No, I don't want anything special."

"We know. But we all want to come over and make a special dinner for you. Just Rachel, Paul, Zeke and myself. Of course, if there's anyone you want to invite…"

"No, that sounds perfect. You know I don't like attention."

"Good. We'll come over in the early afternoon and put together your favorites. Is it okay if Rachel stays the night? She'll need to fly back to work the next day. And Zeke has a special surprise for you."

Ivan's birthday came and his daughters, son-in-law, and grandson arrived shortly after 1:00 with boxes of food and drink. Rachel hadn't seen her father for over a year and was the first to hug and accept a kiss on her forehead. The first thing Ivan noticed was how tall Zeke had become. It had only been a few months, but he seemed a foot taller and his voice was noticeably raspier when he said, "Hi, grandpa."

His daughters made him his favorite lasagna with garlic bread and a tossed green salad dressed with Marie's blue cheese dressing. They poured a quality Chianti wine, even allowing Zeke to sip a bit from Ivan's glass.

"We have apple pie for dessert, dad," said Annabel. "But first your surprise. Go ahead Zeke."

"Grandpa, for your special birthday gift, we'll need to go over to Cynthia's house. She has a special performance planned just for you on grandma's Steinway."

"Dad, Zeke arranged this all my himself. We'll have the pie over at the Berkowitz's."

"Zeke, I can't think of a better present."

Cynthia opened the door and invited Ivan and his family to come in and sit in folding chairs that had been arranged around the Steinway, which filled the living room. Cynthia's parents stood on the other side of the piano along with Dr. Semenov.

"Happy birthday, Ivan," chorused the Berkowitz's and Dr. Semenov. "This is a special one and we hope to add to that specialness tonight," said Dr. Semenov. "We've planned several Chopin pieces for you."

"You know how much I love Chopin. I think it's how Isabel and I best communicated…through music more than words. "Ivan, I have two of my best students ready to perform for you tonight. First, Zeke, please begin." Ivan sat stunned as his grandson stood and sat at the piano bench. He looked at Ivan, smiled and began to play Chopin's Prelude in E-Minor (op.28 no. 4). He played with the same precision and touch as Isabel. The music flowed and caused Ivan to close his eyes with his hands folded under his chin as he drifted into pensiveness. A few tears welled and dripped down his cheeks.

"How did this happen?" Asked Ivan when Zeke had finished.

Annabel answered, "When Zeke was old enough to learn, mom began his lessons. Zeke showed an amazing talent very early on. Mom didn't want you to know. She swore all of us to secrecy. She wanted Zeke to own his talent and only let you know when he was ready. When mom became ill, she contacted Dr. Semenov who immediately said he'd take Zeke under his wing." Ivan was speechless. There was a short period of silence while everyone looked at him with caring smiles.

"But what piano did he play. Isabel insisted that the Steinway be given to Cynthia."

"We have a Yamaha baby grand at home. Sometimes Cynthia would come to our house and take a lesson with Zeke."

"Grandpa, I wanted to give you a present you would always cherish."

"Ivan," said Dr. Semenov, "your grandson inherited Isabel's gift and I believe he and Cynthia have wonderful careers ahead."

After an hour of expertly played preludes and nocturnes, Ivan and his family walked home. While Annabel and Paul gathered up their things, Ivan took Zeke aside. "I am so proud of you. I only wish your grandmother could have been here tonight." Zeke hugged Ivan and accepted the kiss on his forehead.

"Grandpa, I can't explain it, but I feel grandma's presence whenever I play."

"I know, Zeke. I know exactly what you mean."

After Annabel, Paul and Zeke left, Ivan sat on the back porch. It was a warm evening, and he savored another glass of Chianti. A few minutes later, Rachel joined him on the porch. They sat quietly for a few minutes before Ivan said, "I'm sorry."

"For what, dad?"

"Just sorry." Ivan took Rachel's hand and continued, "Thank you for today. I love you very much." Rachel stood and leaned over Ivan to give him a kiss on the forehead.

"Good night, dad."

Ivan sipped his wine and stared up at the clear, moonless sky. Eighty still brought surprises and great joy. He could hear Chopin. He felt

Isabel nearby.

"Izzy, you kept a secret from me."

"I wanted Zeke to have his own dream."

"I understand, Izzy. I took yours away. I'll always regret it. But why give away the Steinway?"

"The grand piano lives within Zeke. And that's enough."

"And so, do you, Izzy. So, do you."

Ben

As he pulled off the freeway, he thought about what his mother had said as she hugged him goodbye. Whenever he left after a pleasant or unpleasant visit, Ben's mother always had some sort of sticky cryptic message that haunted him on the ride home. She was, after all, a self-appointed "omenist", a word she had coined to describe her "powers of knowing the future before the future revealed itself." When Ben suggested that the correct word was "seer" or "fortuneteller" or, better yet, "con artist", his mother's placid rebuttal was that she was different from those who professed special powers, and that omenist would prove to be the better term. His mother made no claims to know everything about the future. She merely claimed to know that every once in a while, something good or bad might be happening soon. Fortunately, he had become unconsciously competent at downshifting through the Triumph's gears and stopping at the bottom of the exit ramp. Otherwise, being lost in thought would have resulted in multiple disasters.

This visit had been pleasant, unlike the previous one when his mother told him his life was too comfortable. He dropped by unannounced to bring his mother a bag of lemons and limes. After drinking iced tea with some lemon juice and freshly baked oatmeal raisin cookies, his mother hugged him and said, "Ben, just remember that being a man means more than being a man." At thirty-nine, his mother was the only parent he had known. She was three months pregnant when his father was killed by Maoist terrorists while trekking in Nepal, after being warned by his mother that no good could come of hiking in foreign lands. Growing up meant a seemingly endless stream of caregivers while his mother worked two or three jobs to provide him with private schools, guitar lessons, summer camps, the most up-to-date computers, "with-it" clothes, and a diet of mostly organic foods. His mother never took advantage of knowing the future; rather, as she often reminded Ben, she elected to live in the "here and future." She often reminded Ben that it would be unfair to take advantage of one's special gifts to indulge in unnecessary frills or self-indulgencies. After graduation from law school at the top of his class and securing a job with one of the most prestigious San Francisco law firms, he bought his mother a condominium near the Giants new ballpark along with season tickets with his first of many extravagant annual bonuses. His mother loved baseball but could never afford to attend a game.

Ben pulled into his Pacific Heights flat's driveway, pushed the button of the garage door remote control, and quietly thought about all he had accomplished before forty: An Ivy League law education and an exceptionally high seven figure salary. He spurned the offer of partnership, since it would mean too much responsibility for shared oversight of the firm's business, and he already made more money that he could ever spend. He invested well, had all the adult toys he wanted, and was recently named by San Francisco Magazine as one of the Ten Most Eligible Bachelors in the Bay Area. He felt very much like a man on top of the world. His mother, however, always reminded him that the future was not what he made of it; it was what the future made of him that mattered.

As he sat in his sports car, he fixated on a red azalea in full bloom. Ben wasn't a gardener. In fact, he had no interest in gardening. He felt it was important, for the sake of a good image, to have a professional gardener install and maintain the planting beds in front and behind his home. He had spent an inordinate amount of time and money for something he rarely noticed. This particular plant struck him as being perfectly beautiful. The red flowers reminded him of the lipstick his mother wore. They glistened with dusk's moisture. Something to his left broke his rare hypnotic state. He couldn't be sure, but it appeared that it might have been someone running silently across the intersection at the end of the block. He turned and saw another runner carrying what appeared to be a baseball bat. He thought nothing of it and pulled into his garage. Before getting out of his classic sports car, he scanned his mostly empty garage. There were no tools, gardening implements, or any other typical items found in garages showing evidence of home ownership. In one corner stood a folded ping-pong table shrouded in a blue tarpaulin that had been used once for a housewarming party given by one of Ben's law firm colleagues. A dart board randomly stung with six darts hung on the wall to his left.

His garage was a flight of stairs below his two-story home. He entered through the kitchen, threw his keys into the basket that served to catch miscellaneous items for which there were no clear organizational constructs. His home, as were his routines, was organized like an old-fashioned postmaster's desk. Everything had its own specific cubbyhole. The first floor was a large open space that included the kitchen, dining area, living room, and a small powder room. A professional designer had not only furnished it in Ben's post-modern taste but had also equipped it with every essential and non-essential gadget for which she could justify the retail plus consultation fee. Ben did not know that he owned five different types of vegetable peelers, nor did he care to know. It was more important that visitors knew that his Williams-Sonoma furnished kitchen, which included All-clad cookware, six-burner Viking stove, and a Sub-zero refrigerator, stood ready for preparing any dish requiring a state-of-the-art blender, mixer, or cookie sheet. Ben didn't cook, but he had acquaintances and a mother who did. Upstairs were three bedrooms, the smallest of which served as a home office. The master bedroom and bath, along with the living room, had sweeping views of City lights at night and the Golden Gate during the day.

Before shedding his work clothes, he plugged his iPod into the central music system and selected Mozart's Fantasia in C Minor for piano, played masterfully by Glenn Gould. He loved the mixture of serious and playful music and the intensity of Gould's rendering. Ben listened to all music genres except Chinese opera, which he found to be atonal and unnatural. Other than a good wine, music was the only sensory stimulant Ben used to enhance his ritualized lifestyle.

After changing into jeans, sweatshirt, and running shoes, Ben intended to walk down to the bottom of the hill to pick up a newspaper and some gourmet take-out from one of the popular boutique neighborhood restaurants. Intentions change when confronted outside your bedroom door by tall, blond, hallow-cheeked woman dressed in a tan topcoat, flowing red scarf, red watch cap, and large black sunglasses holding what initially looked like a cannon of a handgun.

"Good music choice, now sit down, Ben. You won't be going anywhere for a while."

Ben stood not knowing what to do. The woman again told him in a measured tone to sit down against the wall with his hands behind his back "Close your eyes, Ben. You don't know me, and it would be best if you never do. Close your eyes, Ben." After following her instructions, Ben felt two large patches being placed over his eyes followed by the sound of tape being pulled off a roll. "I'm going to secure the eye patches with duct tape, Ben. After I do, I want you to roll onto your belly while I wrap your hands with tape. If you try to resist, remember I have a weapon and the ability to use it." Ben did as instructed and was assisted to a standing position. "We're going to go downstairs, now." The lady with the topcoat and gun led Ben down to his living room with the panoramic view of the City lights and seated him in the yellow leather chair he rarely used. She instructed him to sit quietly, ask no questions, and wait for further instructions. He wasn't sure if those instructions would be meant for him or her.

For several minutes, Ben's mind remained blank. He didn't know how or what to think. Slowly he began to meticulously take stock of his situation and try to give it some meaning. He practiced mostly anonymous law. He did research for large class-action lawsuits. He rarely met the individual clients who benefited from his investigatory gifts. The firm's partners understood that Ben's strengths resulted in large corporate profits, and they paid him royally for his efforts. Ben's first thoughts were that no single person could possibly be seeking revenge against him, because he worked for the benefit of large faceless groups. He also had an astonishing track record: he had never been on the losing side. The losers were always, like Ben, anonymous entities—deep-pocket corporations with deep-pocket insurance companies paying damages. He concluded that his circumstance could not be about his work.

He could not imagine any personal relationship to be the source of any violent behavior towards him. He had few close friends and no current romantic relationship. It seemed that being named one of San Francisco's most eligible bachelors was more of a curse than a gift. The notoriety more often than not was a reason for women to shy away from being seen with him. He surmised that celebrity must be the reason for his sudden victimization. Clearly, this criminal act would turn out to be nothing more than crime for profit. He thought that what he needed to do was keep calm, be patient, listen carefully, follow instructions, and gather available information so that he could effectively negotiate a win-win settlement.

His captor had not physically harmed him, and so far, appeared to behave in a direct and business-like manner. Her instructions were clear, direct, and not spoken with vile temperament. Ben thought this must be a professional crime, not some amateurish whimsy. He heard three short, followed by two short, knocks at the front door. "Come in boys," said the woman. "Put the baseball bat in the corner. He's secured. Remember, I'm the only voice he hears. Have a seat on the sofa." Ben now knew that she had colleagues in crime. He didn't know that the two men had been a diversion while he sat in his driveway. They ran across the intersection to pull his attention away from the open garage allowing the woman to enter and hide behind the folded ping-pong table. "We'll wait for the call."

"May I ask what's happening?" Ben said with all the politeness he could fathom.

The woman replied, "You need to sit quietly and wait."

Ben obeyed. A cell phone rang, and he heard the woman answer. "Yes, I understand. Don't you think it may be a bit early for that? Okay, then we'll proceed." He heard the phone click shut. "Ben, I've been instructed to shoot off the small toe on your left foot. I'll be removing you shoe now." This marked the first of what would prove to be several feelings of panic for Ben. Suddenly any thought of rationale disappeared. He felt a shudder spike from the base of his spine up through his shoulders and skull. When his left New Balance cross-trainer was slipped off his left foot and sock pulled off, he discharged a small amount of urine and felt cold perspiration ooze around the collar of his shirt.

"Wait, please," he trembled. "Can't we talk about this? What is it you want? Money? Legal advice? What is it?"

"Ben, I'm sympathetic to your situation, but I've been instructed. We'll talk about what we want after we get your attention and compliance. You have a reputation for believing you can solve anything through reason and negotiation. We'll need to make sure you understand in advance that there will be no negotiation, no compromise, no reasoning. This isn't about being rational; it's about performance on our terms."

Ben heard a mechanical sound that he couldn't identify. "What are you doing?"

"Turning the silencer onto the pistol," was the cool, surgical reply. Then he heard a pop and his entire body stiffened. "That was a test shot. The only real noise from the next shot will be your scream. Most likely you'll pass out. We'll have you treated with an anesthetic and bandage before you awake. We also have pain medication for you."

Ben began to feel cold and nauseous. "Please, can't we talk first? Let's think about future consequences. Let's think about the future," he pleaded.

"We are your only future, Ben. You need to know that."

"I do. I promise. I do." Silence in the room ensued. Ben felt colder and began to shiver. A metallic taste pushed up through his throat and the back of his head began to tighten and ache. "Please," he whispered.

Finally, the woman spoke. She said that while she had been given specific instructions, she did have some discretionary power. She assured Ben that unnecessary pain and suffering could be avoided if he followed all demands. He felt his breathing slow and he consciously took a deep breath filling himself to his diaphragm and gaining some measure of calm. He assured the woman that he would do all as she requested.

"I need you to call your mother, Ben. You must instruct her to come here. The business we have involves her. Once you fulfill this demand, you'll be freed from all other obligations."

"How is my mother involved in this?" The tightening ache pulsating across the back of Ben's skull began to surge down the nape of his neck and spread across his shoulders. "You mustn't hurt her."

"Ben, you have a choice to make. Get your mother over here or suffer painful consequences for not obeying orders. I'm going to hold a phone to your ear and dial her number. It's your choice how you handle this. If you tell her something is wrong, the toe is gone and there will be other serious consequences."

The phone was put to Ben's ear and during the six rings that it took before his mother answered, he thought about options. He could make an outrageous request that might alert her to something being very wrong and subsequently prompt her to seek help. However, he couldn't think of any invented story wild enough to prod his mother to take such action. Of course, he could also simply blurt the truth of the matter and suffer whatever consequence might ensue. He chose instead to engage in conversation while trying to buy time to figure out another solution.

"Mom, you said something when I left this evening that I've been wondering about. Do you remember?"

"Yes, Ben. I told you that being a man was more than being a man. Is that why you've called?"

"It's just that from time to time you say things that leave me wondering. Like being an omenist and knowing what the future brings."

"But, Ben, I don't know what specifics the future holds. I only know if the future might sustain promise or hold potential doom. What's bothering, Ben? You sound down."

"I still want to know what you meant about being a man." The phone was removed from Ben's ear and he heard it being hung up. The woman told Ben to stop stalling and get to the point. Ben explained he had never spontaneously asked his mother over to his house and that he needed to find a way to do so without raising suspicion. The woman agreed and explained that she would redial his mother. She instructed Ben to say he accidentally disconnected the phone. Once back online, Ben again asked what his mother meant about being a man.

"Ben, I felt a presence about the future that would require you to make an extremely difficult decision. I simply wanted you to know that being a man sometimes requires action that benefits others while resulting in undesirable conditions for the one taking action." His mother's response seemed rehearsed. It appeared to Ben that his mother was trying to teach him a life lesson. The tightness in his shoulders increased, perspiration soaked the collar of his sweatshirt, his right eyelid began to twitch, and he felt a shiver and fainted. His captor, while holding the phone in her left hand, used her right hand to push Ben against the back of the yellow, leather chair and keep him from tumbling forward. Her accomplices moved to hold Ben back by the shoulders. The woman took the phone and matter-of-factly told Ben's mother that Ben would be calling back soon.

When Ben regained consciousness, the woman offered him a sip of room temperature water. Ben sensed perspiration dripping down his spine and soaking through his sweatshirt. The woman observed color returning to his cheeks. What she couldn't see was that Ben awoke with a new sense of self and resolve. "Ben, you must call your mother again. You'll need to explain that a friend suddenly dropped in and apologize for hanging up so abruptly. Do you understand?"

Ben replied, "I need more information. You can do whatever you want to me. I don't really care. But you need to tell me how my mother is involved before I decide what I'll do next. Go ahead: shoot off my toe."

The next time Ben came to was in an ambulance. His left leg was elevated, and he felt a throbbing pain from where his toe had been. "You're lucky," remarked the EMT. "Whoever shot you had some medical expertise."

The policewoman riding with the EMT informed Ben that an anonymous caller made a 9ll call from his house to report the incident. She explained that he was found on his back, eyes patched, and his leg elevated on the leather chair. "Whoever did this to you was careful to minimize physical damage."

Ben asked the policewoman to call his mother and tell her what had happened. "We've already contacted her. She'll meet us at the hospital."

Max

Max lived a simple life. The small closet in his one-bedroom apartment reflected his minimalist beliefs. Long-and short-sleeve blue and white cotton dress shirts, tan pants, two blue and three black blazers, one navy blue suit, seven red ties, and three pairs of dress shoes made up his entire work wardrobe. For weekend wear, there hung two pairs of Levis, four T-shirts, one V-neck black sweater, one red cardigan sweater, a yellow and green Hawaiian shirt given to him by his mother on his thirty-third birthday, a pair of all-white New Balance sneakers and a pair of flip flops. At six foot four and exactly two hundred pounds, Max's clothes hung loose and straight, and, to his colleagues at the small college at which he taught English literature, seemed perfectly in keeping with his personality.

Every morning at precisely 5:30 AM, National Public Radio woke Max. He would remain in bed through the news update, then rise, slip into his jogging clothes, and run the same three-mile loop he had run for the past five years. After shaving and showering, a breakfast of rye toast, vanilla yoghurt, three stewed prunes, black tea, and a multi-vitamin, Max would read the New York Times and five poems from the frayed Norton Anthologies he had first used as an undergraduate at the same college where he was now a tenured full professor. At thirty-five, he was the youngest tenured professor at this Midwestern, ivy-covered college.

Students enjoyed Max's classes. They found his lectures interesting and the questions he posed intriguing. The serious students imagined Max to have a casual and uncluttered academic life. Less serious students fantasized a romantic relationship with him. After all, Max was a handsome man bordering on prettiness. His blonde hair stylishly a bit out of place, bluish eyes that always seemed actively engaged, an easy smile filled with genuine sincerity, and a relaxed gait that made it easy to keep up with him on walks across campus. Acquaintances were never sure if Max's bent was towards men or women. This was a part of his life that Max kept completely private. It might have surprised some to know that he was heterosexual. Although he was not currently involved, there had been five women in his life. And each relationship, with the first being in graduate school, was kept mutually discreet to ensure respect for his lover and privacy for Max.

After completing his daily college duties, Max would stop at the University Diner for dinner. He always sat at the same window booth, which had become known as Max's Booth. Karen Allensworth served him every day except when she had a commitment with her school-aged son.

Max ordered one of three meals. His first choice, if it was fish, was the daily special. Otherwise, it was sirloin tips over egg noodles with a green salad and bleu cheese dressing on the side, or a chicken cutlet without gravy and a cup of the soup-of-the-day, unless it was a creamed soup, and then he would have a green salad with Thousand Island dressing on the side. With his meal, he drank two glasses of unsweetened iced tea with lemon and had one cup of black coffee and apple pie for dessert. After dinner, Max walked to the college library, where he wrote in his journal, read obscure poems, and chatted with the serious students until 9:00 PM, when he walked home and retired for the evening. The only exception to Max's weekday routine occurred on the third Wednesday evening of each month, when he would hold court with interested students at the Village Pub. Over beers, pickled eggs, and pretzels, Max and the serious students would engage in debate over some unresolved issue that had come up in class. On weekends, Max cooked for himself.

It was on one of those Wednesdays when Jill Templeton walked through the pub's front door, purposefully approached Max, pulled a small caliber pistol from her purse, and shot him in the head. Max fell to the floor. Jill Templeton turned and walked out the door to the nearby police station, where she reported her crime and was arrested. In the meantime, an ambulance responded and whisked Max off to the hospital where he lay with tubes and breathing devices keeping him alive. Medical tests determined that he was not brain dead. Apparently, the bullet was not powerful enough to obliterate brain functioning, but it was lodged in a place where it could not be removed.

While Max remained in the hospital, Jill Templeton's trial was a speedy one. She pled guilty and explained that she was one of the few students who had failed one of Max's English literature classes. She told how she had offered sexual favors in exchange for a passing grade but had been spurned. Her attorney convinced the judge that she was clearly a deeply disturbed young woman and ought to be committed to a psychiatric facility.

Thinness was a genetic trait that ran in Max's family. Every day of his hospital stay, his thin, sixty-year-old mother visited from 11:00 AM until 3:00 PM. His thin father had died in a fiery accident as an amateur sports car racer when Max was ten years old. He had no siblings and his mother never remarried. His mother always brought a bag lunch, usually egg or tuna salad on white bread, an orange or apple, and two Oreo cookies. The nurses would bring her apple juice or water, which she drank out of the serving container.

Max did not inherit his imagination. His mother and father led ordinary, plain lives. His father owned a gas station and purchased an extravagant amount of life insurance that served his mother well. His mother never held a job outside their tidy, cottage-style home. She dutifully cared for Max through his undergraduate schooling, and she belonged to the same women's service club for almost forty years. Max's imagination emerged in early adolescence when he began writing poetry. With his father gone, his mother would sit at the dinner table and listen as Max read his daily poems. She would silently affirm his efforts with nods and smiles. His mother never fully understood his obscure metaphors and references. When Max left for graduate school, he and his mother kept in touch with weekly letters, hers mailed on Friday and received by Monday; his sent on Tuesday and received on Thursday. Only visits home on observed holidays broke the routine. Well-crafted words defined this mother-son relationship better than promises and feelings.

While Max lay in his coma, Jill Templeton sat incarcerated in a ten-by-ten-foot room in a psychiatric hospital surrounded by lush woods and a twenty-foot security fence. She was awakened each morning, had breakfast among fifty other criminally insane patients with whom she had no ongoing relationships, attended a one-hour group therapy session, walked the grounds when the weather cooperated, ate lunch with the same fifty criminally insane patients, and retired to her room to spend two hours writing letters to Max. At 3:00 PM she had a one-hour private therapy session with a staff psychologist, at which time she delivered her daily letter to Max hoping it would be mailed. The psychologist dutifully made note of each letter and turned it over to the staff psychiatrist for analysis and feedback. The letters were never mailed.

Jill Templeton could best be described as cute and bouncy. She was twenty-eight, red haired, with a perfect complexion and a slender, well-proportioned body. In high school she was a cheerleader who never dated. She learned early on to sit at the front of the classroom, smile, raise her hand, and reply to questions even if she didn't know the answers. She always stayed after class to ask a question or two. She was what teachers would describe as a polite and ideal student. Although she didn't do well on tests, she turned in all her homework and excelled at participation. In return, she received grades good enough to gain entry into college even though her college entrance exams were below the norm. Jill's parents, neighbors, and friends could not understand why she would shoot a college professor.

They collectively believed that Max must have done something to incite Jill to such gruesome action.

In his coma, Max began to dream. All of the dreams involved Jill. The first was a replaying of Jill walking into the pub. At that moment, Max hadn't recognized Jill, even when he saw her pull the pistol from her purse, aim, and shoot. In his dream, he saw Jill enter in slow motion wearing a pink cashmere sweater, blue jeans, clogs, and carrying a black tote-style purse. He watched her walk towards him, reach into her purse, pull out the pistol, and fire. He saw the bullet leave the barrel and strike him in the forehead. He felt nothing but watched as the serious students screamed; their mouths wide open, and saw Jill turn to walk out the door after dropping the pistol on the black-and-white linoleum floor. Max played this dream like a video loop for months.

Doctors would tell his mother that his brain was still very much alive and that there was evidence from both brain wave activity and rapid eye movements that he was dreaming. They encouraged his mother to talk to Max as much as she was comfortable. She began writing letters to Max and reading them to him later. She would three-hole punch the letters and place them in a binder. She believed that, should he recover from his coma, the letters would serve to fill in the history of his long sleep.

In the meantime, Jill's letters, which had begun as long apologies, were turning into love letters. They began as a simple wooing gesture. She wrote about flirting with Max in class, and how she would answer a question from the lesson's literature assignment by doing what romance novels had instructed: look up from her book with come-hither eyes, moisten her lips with a swirl of her tongue, and softly say that she couldn't remember. She wrote long descriptions of how she dressed to seduce Max. She described a life that they might have together in a romanticized future, and slowly her letters evolved into highly erotic descriptions of an on-going honeymoon. The more Jill wrote, the more connected she felt to Max. She thought of the ink flowing from her pen into Max's veins as a life-sustaining plasma.

Max's dreams about Jill began to change. At first, he heard Jill's apologies as whispers. With each new apology and description of her own condition, her voice became louder and clearer. Max found himself seeing Jill in her own deep sleep—unable to be free of her own circumstances. Max imagined his own letters in reply to Jill's long narratives. He would ask for Jill to clarify her motivation for injuring him. He would describe his own disconnected state and inform—and later remind - her that she was his only link to the outside world. Each new response from Jill brought him comfort. Max grew increasingly sympathetic to Jill's isolation.

As Jill's letters became more sexually explicit, a new video loop in Max's brain took on highly charged romantic overtones. He vividly saw himself and Jill meeting for sexual trysts at fancy hotels and weekend stays at country inns. Evidence of these new dreams showed as increased brain wave activity and visible erections. The dreams grew in intensity for most of the second year of his coma.

Jill wrote ninety-nine letters. Her last letter to Max was a suicide note. In it she apologized again for the pain she had caused. She described her longing for him and the belief that they would one day meet in heaven. On the day Jill hung herself, Max awoke.

Several months later, after undergoing extensive voice and physical therapy, Max was back at the college teaching serious and less serious students. He resumed his regular rituals. One day, he sat at his usual booth at the diner. Only this time he was joined by his mother. She was sharing the binder filled with the letters she had written during Max's hospital stay. Max had ordered chicken noodle soup and salmon patties. His mother chose an egg salad sandwich and an iced tea. As Max flipped through his Mother's letters, he was approached by one of his less serious students. She politely leaned over and whispered into Max' ear. He considered her request and decided to meet with her later in the week.

When Max's mother inquired about the young women, Max informed her that she was the friend of a very dear, departed friend.

Trapped

Trapped. At least it feels that way with a Life Partner, three dogs, two cats, a gerbil and an ant farm. Two of the dogs, both of the cats, the gerbil and the ant farm being looked after while the Kid hitchhikes around the globe on a journey of self-discovery. The Life Partner and I not speaking at the moment due to the continuing argument over who needs to feed what animals at whatever specific feeding times that were dictated by the Kid before she left for worlds-to-be-discovered. The one dog the Life Partner and I share eats whenever he feels like it. So, when the virus hit and we were ordered to shelter in place, things got dicey. And the Kid is quarantined in Peru.

I've heard that resilience is an indicator of good mental health. Well, that might be true. But it's awfully difficult to be resilient when constantly nagged to pick up dog poop, clean out the cat box, and put fresh newspaper...torn into "not-too-wide and not-too-thin" strips...in the gerbil cage. Fortunately, the ant farm is low maintenance. I gave up responsibility for the shared dog several years ago. Resilience...better yet, recovery...seem to be a distant dream.

Then the Kid called. Finally. The Life Partner and I were sitting in the living room reading, the shared dog curled at my feet, and listening to the gerbil spinning away in its cage when my cell phone rang. I knew it was the Kid because of the distinctive ring tone she had installed. "Wild thing, you make my heart sing, you make everything groovy," was the portion of the Troggs 60's anthem that our twenty-three-year-old daughter thought an appropriate way of alerting us to her availability.

"Hello."

"Daddy, is the Life Partner there?"

"Are you okay? What do you need?"

"I need to talk to the Life Partner."

The Kid calls me on my phone, not the Life Partner's, to talk to her mother. Typical.

The Life Partner talks with the Kid for a few minutes, mostly listening with verbal nods, "Uh huh. Yes. I understand. I'll tell him." I watch and listen trying to decipher what sort of plot they are designing against me. The Life Partner hands the phone to me and says with a serious and somewhat caring tone, "She needs to talk to you. Please, listen and count to five before responding."

Count to five? Now I'm beginning to worry. The Life Partner only asks me to count to five when really difficult issues are raised. There was the time when the Kid, who was her high school valedictorian, announced that she wasn't going to college. She didn't see the point. Although she had been accepted to three Ivy League colleges and offered scholarships that would almost entirely pay for a world-class degree, she didn't see the point. At one time, she talked about becoming a doctor specializing in tropical diseases and working in third world countries, but then didn't see the point. She was turning into a raving existentialist and I was preparing to give the fatherly lecture of a lifetime, but the Life Partner said, "listen and count to five before responding." Too often I don't see the point.

"Daddy, I'm scared."

The Kid was never scared. She was fearless. She never backed down when facing a challenge. When she was eight and we were visiting the zoo, she practically begged to get into the lion enclosure. "I want to tame a lion." In middle school she finished Algebra in sixth grade and demanded to take geometry at the high school. Without telling us, she strode confidently into the principal's office and told the Big Boss...her name for the principal...., "You need to arrange for me to take geometry at the high school. It's your responsibility to make sure I get a good education."

"Kid, what's wrong?" Even though her name is Samantha, and her friends and other family members called her Sam, we always called her Kid and referred to her as the Kid. When she was a newborn, I turned to Phyllis and said, "We've made a kid." And from that moment on, we both called her Kid. One of her aunts tried calling her Kid, but she quickly rebuffed that effort with, "Only Mom and Dad get to call me Kid." It was about that time that she also decided that Phyllis would be called the Life Partner. I continued to be Daddy. Life Partner stuck.

"I feel trapped. I'm stuck in a hotel room. I can't leave for any reason. Meals are delivered and left outside my door. I've been told that I could be arrested if I try to leave. Everyone is afraid of the virus, and I'm feeling scared and alone and wanting to come home. Are you and the Life Partner okay."

"We're on a bit of a verbal hiatus at the moment. It seems that we can't agree on how to take care of so many pets."

"How is George, Daddy?" George the Gerbil was the only one of the Kid's pets with a proper name. The others went by Dog One, Dog Two, Cat One, Cat Two, and Ant Relatives in a See-Through World.

"Oh, George is just spinning away and pooping in paper."

"I want to come home."

I could hear the tension in her voice; tiny breaks in what was always a clear and assertive tone. I looked over at the Life Partner and could read concern in her eyes. I wish I could reach through the phone connection, grab the Kid, and pull her home. "We want you here, but there's little we can do at the moment. It's just good to hear your voice. What are you doing in your cooped-up state?"

"I've got my computer and I'm able to do some design work. Money isn't a problem." The Kid was a self-taught graphic designer and web guru. She made plenty of money, which afforded her the luxury of continuous travel. "How are you and the Life Partner doing?"

"We're confined to home, too. We have groceries and other essentials delivered. The Life Partner just signed a pretty hefty book contract, and I had a poem published in another obscure journal." My wife has been a successful mystery writer for over thirty years. I've taught creative writing at the local community college and from time to time have had stories and poems published. So far, I've not received a single cent for anything I've written. The Life Partner inherited the successful writer's gene from her father. I inherited the frustrated artist's gene from my mother.

"That's great Daddy! One of these days you'll get the respect you deserve as a poet."

I hoped that "one of these days" didn't mean posthumously. "Well, at least nobody can criticize my poetry when it's published in an obscure journal that only obscure poets read. Your mother is the writer in the family. Her imagination takes others to unpredictable and engaging worlds. My poetry seems to reside within me with little access by others."

"Daddy, you are my poet."

"Kid, the Life Partner and I really want to help. What can we do?"

"Just listen. Be there for me. I'll get home eventually. And do me a favor."

"What's that?"

"End the hiatus with the Life Partner. She likes your poetry."

'tweener Season

It was one of those days that some call the 'tweener season: still fall but trying hard to become winter. The sun is bright, temperatures cold in the morning, comfortable sweater weather in the afternoon, and all the leaf raking complete. Ralph the mutt stares out the front window watching for dog walkers with their less-entitled pets. Ralph has never been known for humility or refusing any treat thrown his way. He's a six-year-old, 22-pound rescue dog of indeterminate pedigree wondering when he'll get his daily walk. Ralph has a quiet disposition except for his body language. When the leash appears, he's been known to jump and spin with a gymnastic flourish while always sticking the landing.

"Ralph let's go for a walk," magic words spoken by Leon with leash in hand waiting patiently for Ralph to finish a leap and a spin before dutifully sitting. "It looks like a nice day for a walk," says Leon. "Let's walk into town and get some coffee. Maybe one of your friends will be there."

It's about a half mile walk up a short hill and past a newly opened florist shop. Flower boxes filled with a variety of colorful pansies hang below the front windows. However, it's not the pansies that Leon notices when he walks by, but what seems to be the corner of a $100 bill poking up from the damp soil. He pauses and pulls out what appears to be a pristine bill.

"Look at this, Ralph: found riches." Of course, Ralph is more interested in getting back to the walk and to the coffee shop where dog treats are abundant and other canine friends may be present. "I think we'll stop at the bank and check on its authenticity. This may be some kind of a practical joke."

The local Wells Fargo confirmed that the bill was authentic. Leon was pleased and Ralph happily received milk bones, pets and praise from several bank employees. Leon figured that whoever planted the pansies must have inadvertently buried the bill. He decided to stop at the florist shop on the return walk home and inquire if anyone had lost some cash.

They sat at the outdoor patio at Cuppa Joe's for over an hour. Ralph enjoyed more treats and a deep, doggy conversation with an entitled Bichon Frise who had just come from the groomer. Leon stretched his espresso into a second with an almond biscotti while thinking about his newly found cash. On their walk home, Leon paused in front of the florist shop and looked carefully at the box of pansies. Something looked different. He hadn't paid much attention the first time they walked by, but now the pansies seemed a touch larger. This time he noted the vibrant purple and white colors, which invited closer inspection. That's when Leon noticed the corner of another $100 bill poking up through the damp potting mix. He slowly pulled it out and found it to be as fresh and unscathed as the first bill he had collected. Leon looked down at Ralph, who was skilled at maintaining excellent eye contact, and remarked, "Something odd is happening here, Ralph. What do you think we should do?" Ralph cocked his head, which indicated he was either confused or he had some inner understanding of exactly what was happening.

Leon entered Faye's Flowers and noticed a petite, young woman standing behind the counter. She stood with a friendly countenance, sporting short red hair, and with a cheerful lilt to her voice said, "Welcome to Faye's Flowers where we hope our nature improves your nature."

Leon asked sarcastically, "Did Faye train you to say that to all new customers?"

"Actually," replied the store clerk, "I am Faye and I say what I mean."

Leon immediately felt embarrassed and apologized for being rude. "I'm truly sorry. It was wrong of me to make such a comment. Please, know I'm not usually like that."

"Oh, it's okay. I suppose my welcome may have seemed a bit too rehearsed and perhaps a shade insincere, but I'm just trying to grow my business. Pun intended," smiled Faye. As she waved her right arm in a gesture meant to erase any concern, Ralph noticed a tattoo of a purple and white pansy on the inside of her wrist. It dawned on him that it was the same color as the flower box pansies, although the color on her wrist had a certain filmy and translucent quality as though it was a color that had yet to set and become permanent.

"That's a beautiful tattoo on your wrist."

"Yes, I'm partial to pansies. I feel a spiritual connection to them."

"I noticed the pansies in the flower box. Did you just plant them?"

"When I was getting ready to open the store a few weeks ago. Don't you find them to be special?" asked Faye. "Are you interested in purchasing any flowers while you are here? They do improve a home's nature."

Ralph suddenly gave a sharp bark, which was not part of his normal disposition. "Should we buy some flowers?" asked Leon of his companion. Ralph gave another quick bark. "Well, I guess that settles it. How about two dozen tulips?"

Faye gathered a dozen red and a dozen yellow tulips with their petals still tightly closed and explained that they were very fresh and would open soon and last at least two weeks. She also told Leon to add a pinch of sugar and several pennies to the vase with fresh cold water. "They will keep much longer," instructed Faye.

Leon left the shop holding Ralph's leash in his left hand the tulips, wrapped in bright pink tissue paper, cradled in his right arm. He paused to examine the pansies but didn't see any other $100 bills. "I swear these flowers look a little different from the last time I looked," Leon said to Ralph. "What do you think?" Ralph's ears normally sat flat against his square terrier-like black and tan head, but, when asked for his thoughts, they pointed up like triangular radio antennas and rotated a tad towards Leon. Ralph shook his head from side to side and gave a short bark. Maybe it was his way of saying, "Hmmm?"

Leon was not convinced that the $100 bills were legitimate. He wondered if it was possible to fool the bank with an extraordinary forgery. He decided to have a banker examine them again. The next day, when he walked past Faye's Flowers on his way to the bank, he saw that the purple and white pansies had been replaced by pure yellow pansies. They stood proud and were almost iridescent in their yellowness. Leon was reluctant to look more closely to see if there was any money and chose to hasten his walk to the bank. Ralph, however, had a different idea and stopped dead in his four-footed tracks. "C'mon Ralph. Let's get going. You know you like the treats at the bank and then there's coffee." But Ralph wasn't moving. Instead, he turned towards the florist shop's door and pulled Leon in that direction. "Oh, you want to see Faye. Okay, let's go inside."

Faye was at the counter building a mixed flower bouquet and paused to welcome Leon and Ralph. "How are the tulips doing?"

"Just fine," said Leon. "Ralph seems to have grown attached to your shop."

"Is it alright if I give him a treat?"

"Of course."

Faye stepped from behind the counter and bent down to hand Ralph a milk bone. Leon noticed that her pansy tattoo was now yellow. He said, "I noticed you planted new pansies out front."
"No, they're the same pansies I planted weeks ago," said Faye.

"Weren't they purple and white?"

Faye glanced at the tattoo on the inside of her wrist, looked at Ralph, who maintained steady eye contact with Faye and shook his furry head, and said to Ralph, "Did you alter my pansies?" And then to Leon, "I don't think so."

"I would have sworn they were not yellow before, but I suppose I must be mistaken."

Looking back at Ralph, who continued to make unwavering eye contact with Faye, she says, "Your daddy must be imagining things. Would you like another treat?"

Leon has never been a suspicious man. He grew up in a family of scientists. His father taught physics at the local community college and his mother worked as a research chemist. With advanced degrees in information technology, he consulted with several technology companies while working from home. He enjoyed the luxury of establishing his own work routines. He was not one to fall victim to unsupported speculation. He left the unexplained as unexplained unless he had a reason to investigate and find fact-based explanations. He had no use for myths, astrology, religion, or what he labeled as "conjurings to justify the unknown." His intolerance for magical thinking had cost him many shallow friendships and endured him to the deeper ones.

"Well, I guess we'll need to be on our way," said Leon.

Exiting the door and turning left, Ralph stopped and gave a short bark. Leon looked at the flower box and spotted another bill poking its corner from under a yellow pansy. He looked through the window and saw Faye smiling back. He decided he wouldn't pull out the bill. Instead, he tore part of a petal of one of the pansies, which he rolled between his thumb and forefinger as a kind of meditational device.

"Let's go, Ralph. I'm feeling the call of caffeine and a Danish."

Once Leon was seated on the patio at Cuppa Joe's, Ralph went over to say hello and sniff a bit at his old friend Lulu a toy poodle and pug mix with respiratory issues and a forgiving personality. Lulu's owner Penny and Leon were old friends and easily fell into conversation over whatever happened to be the front-page news of the day. Penny was a good listener who asked probing questions and generally held back judgement unless pressed. It didn't take much to press. She had a good repertoire of affirmative nods and encouraging verbal prompts. She and her husband Hugh were avid tennis players. When Hugh wasn't traveling for work, they found as much time as possible to hang out at the local tennis club. When Hugh was away for work, Penny spent as much time as possible at Cuppa Joe's hanging out with Lulu and engaging in conversation with whomever happened by.

Leon shared his experience with what he called the Pansy Flower

Box ATM. Penny listened with a skeptic's brain and an empathetic heart.

"It sounds like some kind of trickery," summarized Penny. "Maybe it's a marketing ploy to generate community interest in a new business."

Leon readily agreed with Penny's speculation and responded, "Well, she's snagged the wrong person to spread the word."

On his walk back home, Leon reached into his jacket pocket and pulled out the torn petal he had thoroughly mutilated while rolling it around between his fingers. In spite of the abuse, it still shown a bright, almost metallic yellow. He decided to stop at Faye's and purchase another bouquet and was happily greeted by Faye. As she wrapped a colorful mixed bouquet, Leon noticed that her wrist's tattoo was missing a petal. A soft residue of yellow made it look like the petal had been smeared away from the whole blossom.

Leon pointed to her wrist and commented, "I guess that's one of those temporary tattoos."

"Not really," said Faye. "I'm not sure why that part seems to have faded. Maybe it's faulty ink."

"I've never heard of that," said Leon. "It seems rather odd." He picked up the bouquet, turned to leave, but Ralph wasn't moving. He pulled on his leash toward Faye. She came from behind the counter with a milk bone in hand and bent over to give it to Ralph, who took it and dropped it to the floor while giving a sharp bark.

"What is it, Ralph?" asked Leon.

Ralph sniffed at Faye's wrist before licking the tattoo.

"Leave it, Ralph. That's not nice."

"Oh, it's okay," said Faye. "It just means he thinks I'm sweeter than the treat."

Leon pulled Ralph away and headed for the door with his bouquet cradled in the crook of his left arm. Again, he paused at the flower box and noticed that several yellow petals had fallen and were already drying and curling. Yet, there was another corner of a $100 bill poking up through the discarded petals. Leon gently pulled it out and found this pristine bill was missing a corner. He quickly folded it in half and pocketed it. "Let's skedaddle, Ralph. Something is not right."

The next day and back at Cuppa Joe's, Leon sat with Penny while Ralph and Lulu visited with sniffs and licks before settling down for their usual naps. Leon filled Penny in on the changes with the pansies, Faye's disappearing tattoo, and the new bill with a missing corner. Penny patiently listened before informing Leon that her curiosity led her to do a bit of research.

"You know that I share your views on myth and religion, but something seemed odd about what's going on with that flower shop," said Penny. "I did a little googling. Did you know that the name Faye means "fairy" and that in some mythology the pansy is thought to be a magical flower?"

"C'mon, Penny, that's ridiculous. We're talking about a well-conceived prank, not some fairytale," said Leon.

"I agree, but it does seem odd."

On their way home, Leon and Ralph were surprised to find the flower shop gone. In just a few hours, all vestiges of the store had been removed, including the flower box, and a "for-rent" sign already hung in the window. An older gentleman was locking the front door and, as he turned, Leon asked, "What happened to the business that was just here this morning?"

"What are you talking about?" asked the round-faced man dressed in a brown tweed suit and sporting a bright yellow silk ascot and matching Tam O'Shanter. "I represent an out-of-town owner, and this store has been vacant for almost a year. The owner just recently asked me to put it up for rent. Are you interested?"

"There was a florist shop here for several weeks. It was here this morning when I walked by."

"Not to my knowledge and the inside is clean as a whistle," said the diminutive man with ruddy cheeks. "You must be mistaken."

"I don't think so. At any rate, I guess it may have been an illegal situation. I'm curious, where does the owner live?"

The pleasant gentleman offered a closed-lipped smile and replied, "Oh, he lives in Ireland."

Samson Lets Go

Samson is a small dog with a big heart, hearty bark and the delusion of persuasion. A black and white rescue dog of mixed parentage; he acts taller than he stands, is attentive to every distraction that comes his way... especially when accompanied with a cookie, and never leaves Wilson's side, his faithful and obedient human companion.

Wilson likes to tell his friends that he found Samson when he and his former girlfriend Colby went to the animal shelter so that she could look for a new pet. Her older cat had lived a long life, and Colby impulsively decided she needed a dog. Wilson thought that it was a funny thing about folks who thought they needed a dog. They don't consider that it's the dog who needs a person. Wilson believed that most pet fanciers were narcissists who sought approval from a creature without fear of rejection. As it turned out, Wilson's professed beliefs proved false and his own need to dote on a pet ultimately led to his split with Colby. He, not Colby, ended up bringing a dog home from the shelter that day.

Colby didn't find a dog to her liking. She wanted a pug or a terrier. She was adamant about her preferred breed. When they walked by Samson's kennel, Wilson paused, Colby made a dismissive remark and urged Wilson to move along. However, Wilson ignored Colby while Samson approached, licked Wilson's outstretched hand and that was all it took. Wilson paid the fee and took home a fifteen-pound, three-year-old dog with a long, wagging tail and a tongue that hung from his mouth like a flexible magic wand. From day one, Samson was always with Wilson. The relationship with Colby ended the moment Samson began receiving all of Wilson's attention and Colby didn't.

The only other dog Wilson ever had was when he was five-years old. His father brought home a black and tan beagle pup who grew to be a burrowing machine constantly digging out of the backyard and often being escorted back from points unknown by the neighborhood motorcycle cop. Officer Mike always carried bits of bologna in a plastic bag to lure Tiger to him on his once or twice a week mission to find and return the happy-go-lucky dog. Wilson and officer Mike were the only ones who found Tiger's behavior endearing and amusing. The final straw for Wilson's dad was when Tiger chewed up an expensive transistor radio along with an envelope containing the week's grocery cash. Wilson's father was determined to take the recalcitrant and unrepentant dog to the pound, but Officer Mike agreed to adopt him. Afterall, they had already developed a kind of bait and love relationship. Officer Mike also offered to arrange for supervised doggy visits. Wilson and Tiger maintained a friendship till Wilson was a teen and Tiger an old dog.

For the next twenty years, Wilson was pet free. He never felt the need to have a furry companion until Samson changed that. Wilson owned a small men's clothing store where foot traffic paid the rent and online sales afforded him a good life. Samson had become a fixture at the store and helped to pull in customers looking for a friendly wag and a facial lick. Wilson always took an afternoon coffee and snack break, leaving his two employees in charge, and walked Samson over to Cuppa Joe's, where they could sit on the patio and meet up with friends both human and canine. Leon was often there with his dog Ralph and sometimes Penny was there with Lulu.

On one particular Tuesday, a sunny spring day with the tree-lined avenues looking like an amusement park ride of shaded green, Wilson and Samson sat with Leon and Ralph. Samson and Ralph had never developed much of friendship and were highly competitive for the treats frequently offered by Cuppa Joe's employees. Leon was Wilson's source of community news. His work life was less structured than Wilson's, which gave him greater freedom to wander about town at hours of his choosing, where he used his exceptional listening skills to acquire an ongoing oral history of all that made their small town an interesting place to live. For years, the local newspaper...a weekly periodical filled with vanity stories submitted by self-promoters, paid advertisements, regular updates from the city council and school board, required legal notices, obituaries (which no one read because everyone seemed to know everyone else) and a few staff-written stories...tried to lure Leon to write a weekly "What's Happening" column. Leon resisted the opportunity by saying that his knowledge was for "conversational purposes only."

Leon shared his fantastical story of finding $100 bills in a planter of pansies outside what was claimed to be a non-existent florist shop. "The shop was there and then it wasn't. A jolly Irishman was putting a "for-rent" sign out the last time I walked by and told me there had never been a flower shop there. Very strange goings on, indeed," related Leon. "But that's old news. Did you hear what happened to Penny and Lulu?"

Lulu, an unusual mix of toy poodle and pug, had seemingly escaped from her backyard and hadn't been seen for days. "Lulu isn't anything like Samson, who never leaves your side. She's an independent pooch who craves adventure. Penny is offering a large reward for her return. What concerns me is that Lulu disappeared the same day as the florist shop, which the Irishman claims never existed. Lulu simply disappeared."

Wilson asked, "You think they're connected?"

"I don't believe in conspiracies, but this seems too coincidental."

"I think we need to do something," said Wilson.

Penny was beside herself. Her husband was away on business. There was nothing unusual about that; he traveled extensively and was gone most of each month. Penny and Lulu wandered a house too large for two people and a small, energetic dog. They often spent time at Cuppa Joe's engaging with other dog lovers who frequented the coffee shop looking for human companionship and doggy socialization. Penny did not fit the stereotype of looking like her dog. She was attractive with a countenance described by her husband as French with a wisp of Danish. He often referred to Penny as his "sweet pastry." Penny thought of it as endearing as long as it wasn't used in public. Penny was also known as an exceptional listener, while Lulu had the reputation of feisty barker. She frequently interrupted conversations and was reluctant to cease her racket until satisfied that she had completed her noisy statement.

Penny had returned home from Cuppa Joe's, put away a few groceries she had picked up on her way home, and let Lulu out to the backyard. Lulu enjoyed basking in the sun on the back porch. When Penny went to let her back in, Lulu was nowhere to be found. Never had Lulu left the backyard and gone off on her own. The large backyard was completely fenced and there were no apparent openings that even a small dog could squeeze through. The three gates were all closed and securely latched. Penny walked her neighborhood calling out for Lulu without success. She knocked on neighbors' doors asking if anyone had seen Lulu. It was still early enough that most of the neighborhood was still at work or school. The few who answered their doors were not helpful, nor even very empathetic. Such was the life for many of her elite and entitled neighbors. She called her husband and felt some relief that he was available, listened quietly while she shared her concern, and suggested she call the police immediately.

"It sounds like a theft. You know there are some folks who prey on animal lovers by stealing their pets and then pretending to find them when seeking a reward."

Penny's spirits dropped even more. She said that calling the police was the right thing to do. "I'm still going to put up some flyers around town and will offer a reward."

Her husband agreed that it wouldn't hurt but cautioned about being taken advantage. "You might want to ask one of your Cuppa Joe's friends to help." The next day, Penny was posting a flyer on the public bulletin board in front of Emile's Grab 'n Go Market when she ran into Leon and related what had happened. Leon promised to spread the word and also keep an eye out for Lulu.

Filing a police report resulted in sincere promises to keep an eye out and not much more. The flyers produced a couple of calls from acquaintances offering condolences, solemn thoughts and not much else. Leon's promise led to a group of Cuppa Joe's regulars who began scouring the town, calling out for Lulu, asking every passerby if they had seen the dog while showing the picture Penny had provided: Lulu looking straight at the camera with all the confidence a small dog thinking it's a big dog could muster.

Wilson kept the picture on his store's counter and asked every customer if they had spotted Lulu. With all the hubbub generated by Lulu's disappearance, Samson seemed a bit on edge with his unique sense of concern every time a customer picked up and studied Lulu's picture. And then Samson disappeared. After assisting a customer, Wilson returned to the sale's counter and noticed that Samson was not resting on his custom-made, red velour dog bed. Samson never left his bed unless Wilson gave permission, or a known customer was in the store. Wilson called out for Samson and searched his store. No sign of Samson anywhere. He asked his other clerks if they had seen Samson. They hadn't. He left the clerks in charge and took off to look for Samson. His worry increased as he quickly walked the blocks around his store. There was no sign of Samson. Wilson saw Leon standing in front of Cuppa Joe's in animated conversation with Penny.

Leon called over to Wilson, "Have you seen Ralph? He's gone missing."

Wilson darted across the street and joined Leon and Penny, "Samson also disappeared less than an hour ago. What in the world is going on?"

The three of them compared stories, shared how suddenly their dogs' disappearances occurred, the searches completed, yet no sign of their dogs. Lulu had been gone almost a week, Ralph and Samson both vanished at almost the same time within hours of each other.

Weeks turned into a couple of months, and still no signs of Samson, Ralph, or Lulu. Wilson knew Ralph and Lulu to have independent streaks, but Samson was a clinger. Wilson felt an emptiness unlike any he had ever experienced. Longer than usual conversations at Cuppa Joe's yielded little understanding of their shared loss. The mysterious nature of it all was too much to accept. They agreed that they had to have been planned events. Why them? Was it tied to some other intention? Was it a single individual who harbored some sort of collective animosity toward the three of them? They could think of no one whom they would label an enemy; certainly no one who had it out for all three of them. They were friendly folks. They gave more to the community than they received.

Leon was convinced it had something to do with the florist shop that was there one day and gone the next…where he had found $100 bills planted among a box of pansies and a proprietor with pansy tattoos on her wrists who vanished along with what the Irishman claimed was a "never there" flower shop.

"The woman's name was Faye and she had pansy tattoos that seemed to change colors along with the pansies in the flower box. And then the shop was gone, and an Irishman said it had never existed. Lulu disappeared the same day," said Leon. "I'm not hallucinating. It really happened."

Wilson said, "But our dogs disappeared a week later, well after the florist shop and Faye were gone."

"I just think there's a connection," restated Leon and Penny nodded in agreement.

More time passed and spring approached with the calendar page turning to March. Time was not healing Wilson's, Leon's or Penny's deep feelings of loss. They found themselves several times a week sitting at Cuppa Joe's with little animated conversation. Speculation had turned to acceptance without resolution. Friends with their own dogs would stop by their table and ask if they had any new clues even though there had been none in the first place. All there had been was disappearance without explanation. Suggestions made to move on and find new companions were met with universal scorn and the response that their grief ran deep, especially with so many unknowns.

"We need resolution, not simply another dog," said Penny, while Wilson and Leon mimed their agreement by nodding.

It struck Wilson as peculiar that he, Leon and Penny seemed more attached to their dogs than to people. He and Leon were single men who had active social lives, dated frequently, and seemed close to their families. However, it was the loss of their dogs that brought about the deepest feelings of loss. Penny was married and expressed deep love and enjoyment with her husband, but seemed happiest when with, as she referred to her dog, "my true love Lulu." Wilson thought it must be because dogs offered uncomplicated affection. He wouldn't go as far as to say "love."

"Love is far too sophisticated and complex an emotion. Tail wagging is about simple joy without pretense. It's an offering that can't be refused except by the coldest of hearts," opined Wilson one day at Cuppa Joe's. "Maybe it's the giving without any expectation of something in return that endears us to our dogs. I know Samson was simply my pal without me having to be his. Although, I couldn't help but reciprocate with strokes and occasional treats."

Sometimes the unexplainable is best left as unexplained. There are too many mysteries that are just mysteries and not worthy of investigation. Often, we try to give too much credence to coincidence. We waste time trying to find cause rather than simply accepting effect. So, on March 17, while sitting at Cuppa Joe's, almost six months since the Big Unsolved Mystery had occurred, Penny, Leon and Wilson were sitting on the patio under a heat lamp nursing large lattes topped with green whipped cream when, out of seemingly nowhere, Lulu, Ralph and Samson came striding in. Wilson was the first to notice because he was facing their entrance. There was Lulu leading the way and wearing a green collar decorated with images of multi-colored pansies and a four-leaf clover tag dangling below. Ralph and Samson followed with similar colors and tags. All three dogs walked with nonchalant authority as they approached.

At first, Wilson was speechless before he finally pointed and said, "My goodness, look!"

Penny and Leon turned, and each dog jumped onto their respective owner's lap with happy barks and affectionate licks. In unison, Penny, Leon and Wilson blurted, "Where have you been?"

All three dogs looked fit, well fed, and normal. After a few moments, Leon noticed something tucked into a slot in the Ralph's collar. He poked his forefinger in and pulled out a neatly folded $100 bill. Penny and Wilson looked on before examining their dog's collars and also finding $100 bills.

Leon asked, "Is this a dream?"

Barry Vitcov is a retired educator having spent 45 years as a middle school English teacher, school administrator, leadership coach, and adjunct university professor. He lives in Ashland, Oregon with his wife and standard poodle. As a teenager, he fondly remembers his father carrying a small collection of his poems in his billfold and showing them off to friends and customers. Barry was raised in the San Francisco Bay Area where he was privileged to experience the 1960's energy, diversity and music as a high school and college student. While attending San Fernando Valley State College (now California State University, Northridge), he was mentored by Newdigate Prize winning poet David Posner, professor and poet Benjamin Saltman and professor Wallace Graves. The lessons from those three extraordinary teachers have served as a lifelong influence on Barry's poetry and narrative writing. During his educational career, he wrote very little fiction and poetry, as he was immersed in his work. After retirement, he began writing again and continues to hone his literary voice. He has had fiction and poetry published in *EAP: The Magazine, Literary Yard, Scarlet Leaf Review, Vita Brevis, Finding the Birds,* and *The Drabble.* His collection of poetry *Where I Live Some of the Time* was published in March 2021 by Finishing Line Press.

www.ingramcontent.com/pod-product-compliance
Lightning Source LLC
Chambersburg PA
CBHW020236030726
47497CB00009B/3124